TOD OF THE FENS

by

ELINOR WHITNEY FIELD

Edited By EriK Publications

ISBN-13:
978-1545203132
ISBN-10:
154520313X

Contents

TO BERTHA E. MAHONY

in gratitude for her friendship and for the richness of her sympathy and understanding.

CHAPTER I.
THE MINSTREL

AT the beginning of the fifteenth century, England was in a very unsettled condition. Richard II had been deposed, and Henry of Bolingbroke, who was responsible for this deed and who usurped the throne thus left empty, found himself in no wise with a well-ordered kingdom under him. Everything was in upheaval. Some of the nobles rallied around the king, but others offered open resistance to him. The young Prince of Wales, while yet a boy, was set at the head of an army and sent into Wales to quell an uprising led by Owen Glendower, who had chosen this favorable time to try to separate Wales from the rule of Henry IV. While the king and the nobles were thus spending their time quarreling and making war on each other, the townspeople of England were doing their best to settle down and lead their own lives in peaceful pursuits. They were interested in their craft industries, their trade guilds, and the growth of commerce with the outside world.

In the district of Lincolnshire to the north of London and not far in from the coast was a small town which was fast becoming a flourishing trading center. This was the town of Boston.

Far back in the seventh century, St. Botolph, a wise and good man, withdrew from the world to found a monastery. He chose a desolate spot then called Icanhoe. It was on the bank of the Lindis, a tidal river which swept in from the sea four miles distant, inundating the low lands and leaving them again a wide expanse of treacherous fens. Here stagnant pools intercepted the wayfarer and sent him out of his way or even caused the death of the man and horse overtaken by night in their midst. In spite of the isolation of this ancient monastery, as time went on a town grew up around it, which came to be known as St. Botolph's Town. At the time of this story St. Botolph's Town was shortened to Boston, and although the monastery had been destroyed during an invasion of the Danes in the ninth century, on its site the parish church of St. Botolph had arisen, and its fine tower was capped by an immense lantern which sent its rays far out to sea and also across the fens to west, north, and south, so that it was a guiding light on that dangerous coast.

Boston was surrounded by high and thick walls fortified with turrets and bulwarks. It was reached from the main highway to Lincoln by a rough road through the morasses which terminated in a big wooden bridge across the Lindis River, now called the Witham. The outer gate or Bridgegate, was in disuse at this time, but the inner one, St. Botolph's gate, was inhabited by a porter whose business it was to collect toll of all who entered this way with merchandise. Market days and fair days were busy days for him, and by night his bag was heavy with farthings and pennies, but other days not many passed into the town. Occasionally there would be a knight attended by his squire who perhaps might be looking for some rich burgher's daughter whose marriage portion would be worthy of weighing against his lineage and knightly reputation; sometimes a group of monks on muleback would ride out on a pilgrimage; and always and ever there were rascals of one kind or another, for the world was full of them and they traveled in many disguises.

Of all who came and went Simon Gough kept note, as he hastened out from his dim, stone-walled room in the gatehouse at the sound of approaching steps. Simon Gough was in the service of Sir Frederick Tilney, who was warden of the bridge appointed by the king. In return for permission to collect toll Sir Frederick was pledged to keep the bridge in good condition, and this he had honestly done. He was the head of a Boston family of good tradition. The Blackfriars monastery which now spread from Shodfriar Lane to Spain Lane, a space of some ten acres, was founded at the end of the thirteenth century by a member of the Tilney family, and the cornerstone of St. Botolph's church itself was laid in 1309 by Dame Margery Tilney. Again and again in important events in the growth of Boston, the Tilney family had figured, and to-day Sir

Frederick held the high position of Mayor of the Staple, for Boston had been made a staple town. This meant no more than that it was one of the towns authorized by the king to be a depot for the export of wool, sheepskins, and English leather. Hence to Boston came foreign merchants to buy, and they were known to the townspeople as "Easterlings," and were looked upon with suspicion.

On a night in early April Simon Gough was awaiting the setting of the sun before shutting the great oak gate, heavily barred with iron. He stood in the archway, his feet wide apart, looking down the road to see if he could spy any traveler who might be headed toward the town. If one should in another moment appear around the wall of the Whitefriars convent, which was laid out with its buildings, orchard, and gardens on the west side of the Lindis, there would time for him to make the town. If he were five minutes later, he would have to seek shelter at the monastery or in some peasant hut on the ridge beyond.

Even as he stood there in his coarse burel tunic with dagger at his belt, a man did appear around the monastery wall and approach the bridge. He wore the flowing gown and hood of a friar, and he was hurrying clumsily, showing that he was aware of the need for haste.

As he set foot on the bridge, Simon addressed him.

"Good even, holy brother; if thou hadst been one moment later thou wouldst not have been greeted by my ruddy countenance with the sun shining on it, but by the blank faces of Sister Oak and Brother Iron. Hasten or they will pinch thy heels."

The friar who stumbled hastily through the gate wore the habit of the Black-friars or Dominican brotherhood, consisting of a black mantle under which could be seen a white tunic, a black hood, and a scapulary, which fell far over the shoulders.

"Good even to thee, good Simon; thou art as prompt in the discharge of thy duties as we who serve a greater Master than thou!"

Simon scrutinized him more closely when he spoke his name. "I prithee do not 'good Simon' me, for I know thee not. At least," he hastened to add, "I should not say I ever before saw that face behind a friar's hood."

The friar did not stop but called back over his shoulder, "God will send blessings thy way if thou but continue to discharge thy duties."

Simon watched him out of sight and until his sandaled feet could no longer be heard on the cobbled street.

"Well, it is no business of mine," he muttered, as he turned to draw the heavy gate to, with a clanking of chains and bolts, "but it certainly does seem as if I always saw that face coming in through the gate and never going out." Sitting down for a minute on the lowest step of the gatehouse, he picked up what he thought to be a flat stone, and making a long mark on the cobble in front of him, he muttered, "Yesterweek it was in a peasant smock sitting on a mule

"GOOD EVEN TO THEE, GOOD SIMON."

with a bag of grain slung in front of him." He made another mark on the stone. "Two days later it was on a chapman who was loath to give me a farthing for his pack." Another mark was drawn on the stone. "Two days ago it was in a minstrel's garb, and now there it goes in a friar's habit, and it's not Simon Gough who makes a mistake in faces. Moreover he did not walk as though he were used to the flapping of cloth around his legs."

He threw the object he held carelessly against the wall of the gatehouse, but it bounded back again to his feet with a metallic sound, and he stooped to pick it up.

"By our good St. Botolph, who am I to be throwing away a gold noble? If these be the blessings that will come my way, far be it from me to go out of that same way to pursue trouble, be it garbed like the Evil One himself." He rubbed the money on his sleeve, and removed the dust which had dimmed its brightness and made it seem no more than a worthless stone. Plainly enough on one side appeared the outline of the ship in which stood the king holding sword and shield, and on the other, the letter and cross surrounded by small crowns and fleur-de-lis.

Chuckling at his good fortune, Simon stowed the coin in his pouch, took down the great iron key from a ledge inside the door, locked the guardroom, and betook himself into the town.

Entering the town from St. Botolph's gate one did not really encounter many signs of life until the main street led into the market place. On one side were high walls enclosing an ancient nunnery and on the other the blank wall of Bailiff Hugh Witham's home, a three-story house of timber, which faced toward Bargate. In the center of the market place was a market cross, a large one with a square tower. From all sides, alleys, well packed with houses whose gabled fronts all but touched across the narrow way, tumbled into the market place. In front of the "Golden Fleece" tavern which stood opposite the parish church, many of the townsfolk had congregated this evening. There were aldermen in scarlet gowns; merchants, clerks, and craftsmen in sober colors; and a group of young men in the latest court fashion, gay in purple, orange, green, and blue. As Simon drew near, he saw that a minstrel was the center of attention, and he hastened that he might not miss the song.

The minstrel's voice rang out clear and mellow. His face was in half shadow, for he stood leaning against the frame of the tavern doorway, so that those who were sitting at the big table within might hear as well as those without. Flickering rushlights played upon the whole scene, making faces ruddy and pale in turn and pewter tankards gleam and grow dull. The odor of ale hung heavy under the low rafters.

It was the noble Moringer within an orchard slept,
When on the Baron's slumbering sense a boding vision crept,
And whispered in his ear a voice, "'Tis time, Sir Knight, to wake,
Thy lady and thy heritage another master take.

"Thy tower another banner knows, thy steeds another rein,
And stoop them to another's will thy gallant vassal train;
And she the lady of thy love, so faithful once and fair,
This night within thy father's hall, she weds Marstetten's heir."

Simon looked around him. All eyes were fixed on the minstrel, who was clad in a green doublet with flowing sleeves, and red hose. The silver chain with the badge such as was common for a minstrel to wear to show to what house he belonged, gleamed on his breast. It was a long story which he had to tell, but the townsfolk did not tire of it. Only the young noblemen tittered occasionally or nudged one another as if this was but poor amusement in comparison with what they were used to at court.

Verse after verse followed. The Moringer, a powerful baron, had set out on a pilgrimage to the shrine of St. Thomas, but before going had called together his vassals and offered his castle, dominions, and lady to the one who would pledge himself to watch over them until the seven years of his pilgrimage were ended. The seven years except for a night and a day were passed, when he was warned in a vision that his lady was on the eve of marriage to Marstetten, the very vassal who had taken upon himself the trust. By a miracle of St. Thomas, the Moringer was able to gain his domain before it was too late.

He leaned upon his pilgrim staff, and to the mill he drew,
So altered was his goodly form that none their master knew,
The baron to the miller said, "Good friend, for charity
Tell a poor pilgrim, in your land, what tidings there may be!"

The miller answered him again, he knew of little news
Save that the lady of the land did a new bridegroom choose;
"Her husband died in distant land, such is the constant word,
His death sits heavy on our souls, he was a worthy lord."

Unrecognized, the pilgrim gained admission to the wedding feast, and drop-

ping his nuptial ring into the goblet of wine with which he asked the lady to pledge her venerable guest, he made known his presence to her and to Marstetten.

It was the Marstetten then rose up, his falchion there he drew,
He kneeled before the Moringer, and down his weapon threw;
"My oath and knightly faith are broke," these were the words he said,
"Then take, my liege, thy vassal's sword, and take thy vassal's head."

The noble Moringer he smiled, and then aloud did say,

"He gathers wisdom that hath roamed this seven twelvemonths and a day.
My daughter now hath fifteen years, fame speaks her sweet and fair;
I give her for the bride you lose, and name her for my heir.

"The young bridegroom hath youthful bride, the old bridegroom the old,
Whose faith was kept till term and tide so punctually were told,
But blessings on the warder kind that oped my castle gate,
For had I come at morrow tide, I came a day too late."

When the minstrel had finished, there was a stir of general approval and an opening of pouches, for all were glad to give a penny or two for such fine entertainment. Tucking his harp carefully under his arm, the minstrel picked his way among the bystanders, collecting the coins in his silken hood.
When he reached the group in which Simon stood, Simon was taken aback with astonishment. Here he saw again the straight nose, high cheek-bones, and bright blue eyes under shaggy eyebrows which he had only a short time before seen in the friar's hood. He passed his hand in bewilderment over his own eyes. Then he opened his pouch as the minstrel stood beside him, but instead of withdrawing his hand with the penny he sought, he stared in amazement at a second noble which appeared in it as the minstrel passed by him, singing the last two lines of the ballad he had just finished.

But blessings on the warder kind that oped my castle gate,
For had I come at morrow tide, I came a day too late.

CHAPTER II. ENTER TOD OF THE FENS

"GOOD MORROW!" said a tall man, stepping out of the wayside bushes and addressing a beggar who came along a rough path that ran beside the Lindis River. "Art thou on thy way to Boston?"

"Ay," was the surly answer, and the beggar turned aside to adjust a patch over one eye, for he was taken unawares, and had been enjoying the sight of the eye that needs must be blinded when he plied his trade.

"Such a poor beggar as thou deserves much pity. I see thou art blind in one eye, poor soul. May St. Catherine heal thee! I suppose thy purse be as empty as thy poor pate. Out with it and let me see!"

The tall fellow who spoke wore a tawny-colored jerkin with loose sleeves of blue and scarlet and stout leather leggings. His head was uncovered and his hair grew heavy and almost to his shoulders. His broad frame and the stout staff which he carried filled the narrow way. The beggar began to whimper and to try to hide his leather wallet that hung among his rags.

"Out with it!" commanded the man again, "for I am loath to lay hands upon thy dirty rags! Seest thou this hand." And he held up his right hand, which bore a deep scar as if pierced through by a dagger. "Take off thy patch that thou mayst see the better. Know then, that that means I have wounded a man, and what a man does once that can he do again an he would."

In those days a man who was caught having wounded another, had the choice of paying a heavy fine, of being imprisoned for a year, or of having his hand pierced by the weapon that did the deed. Without more ado, the beggar loosed his wallet, and turning it up gingerly shook a few farthings and pennies into his hand.

"Up with it, man, and show me the bottom."

The beggar, thus urged, turned up the wallet, the coins filled his hand, and a few fell over to the ground. The beggar made a quick movement as if to recover these.

SOME OF THE BEGGAR'S COINS FELL ON THE GROUND.

"Nay, leave them be," was the curt order. "Now put the rest back in thy wallet and be off before I have a change of heart."

The beggar did as he was bid with more speed than he had yet shown in carrying out any command, and soon he disappeared around a bend in the road, where he concealed himself in the bushes.

"Mayhap he will not find the farthing that rolled into the grass," he thought, as he hid himself to wait.

After a little while he cautiously peered around the curve of the path. No one was in sight, so he advanced slowly and warily. Having gained the spot where the disaster took place, he stopped in amazement. There on the ground lay every groat, penny, and farthing that he had dropped.

Meanwhile the other participant in the adventure walked in the other direction. He walked lightly and whistled as he went. Occasionally he stopped whistling and laughed until the tears ran down his cheeks. "The world be full of fools," he muttered. "How they toil and sweat and cheat and lie for a handful of dirty coins! Well, I have but this right hand to remind me that I once was a fool, too, but thank God I am no more. Heigh-ho! a good tale to tell the band this even."

He had gained a rise of ground and stopped a moment to look around him. Behind lay the great stretch of fens with St. Botolph's steeple rising beyond them and against the sea. Below wound the sparkling Lindis like a silver ribbon through green meadows and pasture lands where flocks of sheep grazed, and here and there could be seen the thatched roof of a peasant cottage.

"Aha!" laughed he. "There is the wretch even now groveling for his money. I knew he would be back to have a look, and I wager he is more surprised than if he found his rags were changed to silk."

He turned again. On the left was the thread of highroad leading to Lincoln and farther on skirting the fringe of Sherwood Forest. Here where the rough country lane joined the highway was an alehouse, as could be seen by the pole with a brush on it which projected over the door.

On the rude bench before the door a man sat drinking ale, who immediately spoke.

"I give thee good morrow, and if thou wilt stop and have a drink with me, all that I ask is to be amused for an hour."

"Thou hast found the right person to do that," was the quick response, "be thou as dull-witted as a mitered abbot, and I can promise thee more than an hour's entertainment if thou wilt do as I bid."

"What is thy name, and whence comest thou?"

"Some men do call me Tod of the Fens and others who are as niggard with their words as with their farthings simply call me Tod, and I care not so long as they shear only my name."

"What meanest thou by that?"

"Alack! where wast thou bred that thou canst not understand a good pun? Dost not know the meaning of 'tod'? It is a good measure of wool and it is this crop of mine that gives me my name," and Tod shook his shaggy head.

"Fetch another pint of ale," called the stranger to the alewife who put her frowsled head out at the sound of voices. She withdrew it and soon appeared with a foaming mug.

Tod seated himself likewise on the bench and drank deeply. Wiping his arm across his mouth, he eyed his companion covertly. He was a young, clean-shaven man with blue eyes deep-set under heavy eyebrows. He wore the livery of some noble, a blue mantle with scarf and hat with cock's feather.

"In whose service art thou?" asked Tod, after his second draught had emptied his mug.

"I am in the service of Tedium and would leave it forthwith. What canst thou offer?"

"If thou wilt take service with me, thou wilt be serving Sir Mockery and a merry time thou wilt have, I promise." And Tod threw back his head and let out such a roar of laughter that the stranger clapped his hand over his ears.

"Hold!" he shouted, "wouldst shatter my eardrums?"

Tod stopped but long enough to take a deep breath that swelled his chest to an amazing degree, and then followed a burst that was second to the other in sequence but not in lustiness.

The stranger dropped his hands and stared. "Egad!" he ejaculated, and then as the laugh died away so that he could be heard, he continued, "If thou canst do better than that last and not burst thyself, I will join thee for a fortnight and a day, that I may learn the art. At the end of that time I should at least be able to pucker this melancholy face of mine into a smile, learning from such an artist."

Tod took up the offer, if one may judge by appearances, for the next moment the alewife appeared, scolding at the disturbance that surely would roil her ale, and only the heels of the stranger were to be seen, for his ears had sought protection in an empty ale barrel which lay on its side not far from the alehouse.

Tod leaned over and pulled up his leather leggings as if they alone had felt the strain of the contortion, and the stranger emerged.

"Thou hast won," he announced shortly. "Now let us be off and see some of these funny things that set thee laughing."

"How now! I was but smiling at thee, and no offense to thee!" said Tod. "It is that serious face of thine that looks as if it would sit better on a prince of the realm than on a keeper of my lord's wardrobe, whose greatest enemy is no larger than a moth."

"Fear not! it is not responsibility that makes me glum but the lack of sport and adventure in this world. I have tried my hand at much, but have found nothing that does not pall ere the froth which it has caused be settled."

Tod rose and shook himself, which was a characteristic movement of his.

"Keep the lid on that smile of thine ere it bubbles up again," cautioned the stranger, "and all that I wish of thee is a twinkle for my eye an it cause not the earth to shake. Come, let's be off!"

"Ay," answered Tod, "off to the fens and to a band of as merry rogues as thou hast ever seen."

"Egad! Will they all smile?" asked the stranger.

"Belike they will if I do not succeed in changing thy countenance before the day is done. I shall name thee Dismas, the penitent thief."

"And pray what have I robbed?"

"Thou hast robbed thy lord of his man and his livery."

"But of that I am not penitent."

"Well, then, thou hast robbed me of my own companionship."

"Ay, truly, and of that I may indeed repent."

So saying, Dismas, as we shall now call him, paid the score and followed Tod out on to the highway. "And how dost thou account for thyself and thy friends?" Dismas continued as they walked along.

"I account for them even as our madcap prince accounts for himself and his gay companions," answered Tod. "At times he is at serious business what with this unsettled state of England, but at other times I hear he gives himself up to mad escapades, now here, now there, matching his wits against those of his subjects. 'Twould do my heart good to match him against my Tom True Tongue, but though Castle Bolingbroke is near, the prince is fonder of London than these parts, and 'tis only occasionally we see even his gay retainers. I might think thou wert one of them indeed, but thou art not gay enough!" and Tod winked a blue eye.

Dismas shook his head. "Indeed I am not one of his retainers nor ever wish to be. The prince, they say, is in truth an odd fellow with a head that would fit a jester's cap better than a crown."

Tod slapped his thigh and laughed. "A man after my own heart then, for it takes a wise man to be a good jester." He put his hand on Dismas's arm, and stopped him on the rise of ground they had just gained. His other hand made a circle taking in the long stretch of fens. "I live in this green stretch of land with the wild birds circling over it. Other men have tired of the false world and have joined me even as thou hast to-day, and we lead a life of outdoor pleasure taking only what is no man's and enjoying what is every man's. Thou wouldst join us for a fortnight and a day, and in that time we shall give thee such entertainment as we have. We ask not who thou art or whence thou comest, for we do know that all men are but wanderers, and the king himself does not rightly know whence he comes or whither he goes. Some men call us idle, but what, forsooth, is idleness? Is it to laugh and be merry, and to be no man's enemy; and is busy-ness to quarrel over gold and silver and be no man's friend?" And Tod again held up his scarred hand. "I quarreled once over gold and silver, but dost think they are worth it?"

"I know not," answered Dismas, "but remember thou art teaching me to laugh and not to puzzle my brains with thy whithers and thy wherefores. Enough of this! Make me laugh ere I gain that oak tree yonder or I'll leave thee straightway and put thee down for a dull companion."

"Marry, I'll make thee laugh then. Answer me this riddle. What is it that walks before thee now, and would walk before even the prince himself?"

"I know not," answered Dismas, "and did I not tell thee I did not wish to puzzle my brains?"

"Ay, that thou didst, but the answer is simple enough, for it is only thy shadow."

"Thou art no dull man, indeed," and Dismas laughed even as they gained the oak tree, "but tell thy riddle to no one else or thou wilt regret it."

"So be it," agreed Tod. "Between thee and me it will rest then."

CHAPTER III. IN THE TILNEY GARDEN

JOHANNA TILNEY was at a favorite occupation; namely, feeding the swans in her father's garden. Johanna was fourteen years old, and if Lady Mathilda, her mother, could have had her own way with her, uninterfered with by Sir Frederick, whose daughter was his most cherished possession, Johanna would now have her hair confined in a jeweled caul with veil attached and her slim waist in a cote-hardie tightly laced, while her gown and hanging sleeves would be sweeping the ground in great elegance. As it was, she was dressed, according to her own wish and that of her father, in a simple, loose gown of Beverly blue which matched her eyes and the reflection of the blue sky in the garden pool, and her short dark hair was caught up under a kerchief.

The swans were pressing eagerly around for the bread crumbs which she was scattering on the surface of the water, and the most forward of the three birds had left the water and was stretching its long neck under her arm from behind, and was stealing the bread from her hand.

"Go to, thou silly bird," chid Johanna, "thou always gettest more than thy share, but thou must work for it if thou wouldst have this bit, and thy greediness will be to thy disadvantage." So saying, she threw the last crust far out into the pond, and with a fluttering of wings, the birds started off to secure it.

As Johanna foresaw, the swan which had come ashore started off quite in the rear, but with a strategic movement it swam off to the right, and when the other birds in their credulity turned to follow, it circled around in front of them and ran off with the prize.

Johanna laughed gleefully. "Thou art not to be outdone. I truly believe thou art descended from that wise swan that belonged to St. Hugh of Lincoln. I'll ask Brother Stephen if this be not so."

It was warm for this time of year as spring had come early, and the fruit trees were about to break into blossom. The Tilney garden was mainly an expanse of soft greensward which stretched away to the side of the house, with carefully laid-out paths wandering among fine old trees; and to the back of the house behind a close-clipped hedge were the kitchen garden and orchard, the larder, the buttery, the brew-house, and the kitchen itself.

The Tilney house was one of the finest in Boston at this time. It was a large one, built of stone and timber. The woodwork was artistically carved with deep scrolls and designs. Each of its two upper stones overhung the one below it, so that the topmost story, roofed in red tiles, leaned out beyond the garden wall and overshadowed the row of small thatched houses that lined the opposite side of the alley, for even as fine a house as this had no other approach than a narrow cobbled lane that was often running with dye emptied from the vats of the dyers who lived and worked opposite. Wide stone steps ran up the side of the house to a terrace and to the entrance to the living apartment which was in the second story.

Having tired of watching the swans, Johanna betook herself to the farthest corner of the garden, where, if her mother was not looking, she could mount the garden wall by means of the strong vines that grew on it and look off across a sloping jumble of tiled roofs and dormer windows to the quay, where many ships rode at anchor, most of them belonging to the powerful Hanseatic League, in the hands of which lay the whole carrying trade of the Baltic Sea. They were vessels of the Hanse, a league of German cities, that sailed from Boston to Bergen in Norway with English wares and brought back cargoes of salt fish, or brought iron from Sweden, wine from the Rhine vineyards, oranges, spices, and foreign fruits from Bruges, and from Russia, wood, skins, and furs. Sometimes there were Venetian galleys to be seen. These were the largest sailing ships of the time, and they had oarsmen, too, that they might move in a calm sea with great speed. To mediæval Europe it was the merchant of Venice or Genoa who hazarded his ships in the mysterious and little known

East, and brought back gems, ivories, spices, and silks.

Near the quay were the warehouses, and here Johanna's father went each day, for it was his duty as Mayor of the Staple to oversee all exportation in these commodities, especially of wool, for that, first weighed at the point from which it was shipped, had to be weighed again at the port of departure, and sealed with the seal of the Mayor of the Staple.

Johanna longed to be a boy that she might take part in the waterside activities, for they held a strong fascination for her, and she plied her father with questions regarding seafaring ways and the lands across the sea. Her father had been to Flanders many times, for the Flemish people were the best weavers in the world, and they were the greatest buyers of English wool.

This morning as Johanna gained her point of vantage, she saw a ship come up the river and anchor in midstream. She knew from the outline of its high stern and prow and the cross of St. George which it flew that this was no foreign ship, but one of the few good English ships that were to be found on the sea, so monopolized by the odious Easterling. Not long afterward she heard her mother's voice calling her, and hastily climbing down, lest she be discovered in her undignified position, she hurried to the house.

Lady Mathilda met her at the door. "Haste thee, Johanna, and dress thyself as befits a young lady of thy age, for thy father has just sent word that he brings a merchant and his son to dine with us. An apprentice brought the message, and at the same time desired the key to the town coffer to bear to thy father. He must be pressed with great matters, and we must see to it that nothing at his home disturbs him."

Lady Mathilda, who was a knight's daughter and had been brought up on a manor in Kent, took great pride in the management of her household and in rich and beautiful possessions. The walls of her home were hung in fine tapestries, and there was much silver plate and carved furniture.

"Thou mayst wear thy best dress sent to thee from London, the rose silk, and also the fine pearl girdle. Now haste thee, for Caroline is even now waiting to help thee."

When Johanna appeared again, she looked like a fine lady indeed, for the gown became her well. Her soft color matched the smooth lustrous silk, and her slim neck carried gracefully the high, heart-shaped headdress of fine linen. Her father and the two guests were talking earnestly when she descended the wide stairway. They were sitting on a carved oaken settle at the farther end of the great hall, and she felt the eyes of the younger one were upon her as she approached. Her father presented her to Sir Richard Branche and his son, Gilbert Branche, both of whom bowed low over her outstretched hand. Sir Richard, like her father, was dressed in a long tunic which reached to the ankles and was buttoned down the entire length of the front. The outer sleeve of the gown was loose and flowing, but the under sleeve was tight and was fastened with buttons to the wrist. This array of buttons and the rich girdle, more ornate than that which her father wore, were what especially attracted Johanna's eyes.

Gilbert Branche was a fine upstanding lad of sixteen, and Johanna liked at once his fresh open countenance and clear blue eyes. They immediately withdrew to the window seat, overlooking the garden, and fell into easy conversation.

"I saw thee when thou didst cast anchor this morning. Hast thou ever sailed up the Lindis before to our town, and whence hast thou come?"

"This is the first time I have ever set foot in Boston, but my father has come often before. We live in Lynn, so it was but a short sail before a good southeast wind."

"And dost thou love the sea?" asked Johanna eagerly, for she knew if the answer were in the affirmative that she would have much to say to this young man.

"Ay," was the quick response, "and dost thou know I have but now gained my father's consent to sail to the Baltic on one of his ships this coming summer?"

"And mayhap thou wilt encounter pirates, for my father says the seas be full of them," gasped Johanna.

"My father is a Merchant Adventurer, and I would be one, too," went on young Gilbert enthusiastically.

At this point Lady Mathilda made her appearance, and the table was laid at the other end of the hall. During the meal that followed the conversation was of many things – the unsettled times, the dishonesty of merchants, and the endless precautions that had to be taken to detect fraud and smuggling, of King Henry and his difficulties with disloyal nobles, of Richard Whittington,

Mayor of London, famous for his wisdom and foresight.

After the meal was over, Sir Frederick and Sir Richard settled themselves down to earnest consultation, Lady Mathilda retired, and Johanna and Gilbert were left to wander through the garden. Gilbert began at once to explain to Johanna just what was meant by "Merchant Adventurer."

"Knowest thou not that England can boast of but a handful of ships to carry on the trade with other countries? We depend upon the Germans, the Venetians, and the Genoese to bring us things and take away our merchandise. Is not that shameful? Why should we not have our ships and sailormen?" Gilbert's eyes flashed.

Johanna watched him with admiration. "Thou art a lad after mine own heart," she answered candidly, "and were I, too, a boy I should be a Merchant Adventurer, if that means sailing far away and bringing back the good things of the world to England."

"Thou must not wish to be a boy, when it is for such as thou that we would brave the dangers and return again. Wouldst thou not rather have thy colors carried across some unknown sea than into a knightly tournament?"

"Ay, truly," answered Johanna.

"Then that will I do, for I have never seen a maid as fair as thou art. Wilt thou have me for thy Merchant Adventurer?" he continued laughingly.

"Ay, truly, if thou wilt be fair and honest in all thy dealings," replied Johanna, "but now come and I will show thee my favorite nook, from which I watch hour by hour the loading and unloading of the boats."

When they reached the garden wall, a look of disappointment came over Johanna's face. "Alas!" she said, "I had forgot that I am in my best dress, and cannot mount. Doubtless, too, thou wouldst not think it becoming in a lady to climb so high. Well, never mind. Do thou put thy foot here, and so on up. I shall stand here and thou canst tell me what thou dost see."

Gilbert mounted the wall, and looked off. "It is a fine view," he called down. "See, I can help thee up, and there is naught here can hurt thy gown."

Johanna needed no second invitation, and in another moment with the help of his hand, she was seated beside him.

"How my mother would scold, should she see me," laughed Johanna delightedly; "but Father would be even as thou art. He likes my daring ways. How pleased he would have been if I had been a son instead of a daughter! Mother thinks only of how she may teach me to conduct myself, so that some good knight will seek my hand in marriage. This summer I am to visit my mother's family, far off in Kent, and there shall I hear of nothing but knights and arms and tournaments. Alas! it will not be to my taste. I like not wars and fighting."

"There will there be so many squires to pay thee court that thou wilt forget this afternoon," and a shadow of disappointment came across Gilbert's face.

"Mayhap," answered Johanna with a coquettish toss of her head and a mischievous smile. "But," she added after a pause, "I do not think so. Tell me some more of the sea. How many ships has thy father, and what are their names, and whither do they go? And look, canst thou tell me whence those ships below come, for that can I tell thee if thou knowest not?"

So the afternoon sped along, until suddenly Gilbert noticed a sudden activity on his father's boat.

"I am afraid that testing of the sail means preparation for departure. We must return to the house and see if my father has already gone to the quay."

So saying, Gilbert helped Johanna safely to the ground, and they returned, still talking busily. Lady Mathilda was the only one within the hall. She seemed to be disturbed.

"I was about to send for thee, Gilbert, for Sir Richard left a short time ago, saying that thou must follow before long. Johanna, thy father is greatly upset. It seems he gave no message to the apprentice to bring the key of the town coffer to him, and he is now trying to seek him out to see what he is about. He does not feel that all is well. Alas! I hope that through my indiscretion no harm has come to the town funds." Lady Mathilda reminded one of a deer at bay, as she walked up and down the hall, her brown silk dress ruffling about her, and her horned headdress towering above her anxious face.

"Did my father know the apprentice?" asked Johanna.

"Nay, he had never seen him before. He said that he turned to a fellow standing near and asked him to carry a message. He did not even notice what he looked like, but that did I. He had bright blue eyes under heavy eyebrows, a straight nose, and high cheekbones."

"Surely one key cannot be enough to unlock the town treasure," said Gilbert. "In Lynn I am sure there be as many as six keys, and each kept by a different person."

"Ay, that is so. I had forgot. The loss of one key is no great concern. I wonder Sir Frederick did not think of that." Lady Mathilda showed signs of great relief. Then after a moment she went on: "The man may have had a special grudge against Sir Frederick. I like not that thought, either. He may think to discredit him in some fashion. It seems to me a most strange occurrence."

"Do not worry, Mother," said Johanna. "I feel sure it is of no great importance. Surely Father's position cannot be shaken by the loss of a key."

Gilbert at this point took his leave, thanking Lady Mathilda for her hospitality and Johanna for the pleasant hour he had spent, and begging that he be allowed to return soon.

"Thou mayst always be sure of a welcome," said Lady Mathilda with great sincerity, for she found that the lad was very pleasing to her, even though she understood from his father that he had decided to go into the merchant trade rather than pursue his knightly training. At least he had served as page and squire in the household of Sir John de Lacy and that was all to his advantage. Lady Mathilda, as much as she honored her husband, still felt a little skeptical of this merchant class that was coming into existence as men of rank and wealth. Surely they would never acquire the honor which fell to the share of the landed nobility.

After Gilbert Branche had left, Lady Mathilda sat down at her distaff to compose herself, and Johanna withdrew to take off her best gown. It was not long before Sir Frederick returned, and his face showed no sign of trouble.

"Hast found the key?" demanded Lady Mathilda delightedly.

"Nay, I bethought me, after I left, that it could do the rogue no possible good. The council meets to-morrow, and then will be time enough to see to getting another key. Meanwhile I have much of interest to tell thee. Where is Johanna? It concerns her not a little."

Johanna had already heard her father's voice, and had hurried down to hear what news he brought. Sir Frederick threw himself down in the high-backed chair, and Johanna perched forthwith on the arm.

"What didst think of the young Gilbert Branche?" Sir Frederick smoothed his short beard with one hand and looked at Johanna quizzically.

Johanna blushed and cast down her eyes. Then feeling that she must say something, she looked up. "Father, didst ever see so many buttons as Sir Richard wore? Why dost thou not have buttons on thy tunic as well as fine embroidery to edge it?" and as she spoke she picked up the edge of his long sleeve and fingered it.

"Sir Richard is a rich merchant and an honest Englishman, which is the highest praise can be given any man. He owns a small fleet of ships, and it is of that that I must tell thee. He has persuaded me to go into a venture with him, and I have even to-day ordered a ship to be built. What thinkest thou of that?"

"Oh, Father," gasped Johanna, "it is the best news I have ever heard!"

"How does it come about that thou, a Merchant of the Staple, canst unite with a Merchant Adventurer?" asked Lady Mathilda anxiously.

"True enough," answered Sir Frederick, "it does seem as if we should be sworn enemies!"

"And why?" asked Johanna, startled at the idea.

"Because, child," answered Sir Frederick, "the Merchant Adventurer is interested in the growth of homemade articles as he can export only those, whereas we Merchants of the Staple do not wish the wool, for example, to be made into cloth in this country as our interest lies in the exportation of raw wool. Dost not see the conflict?"

"Then why – " began Johanna again, but Sir Frederick went on:

"The time is close upon us when the conflict will be fiercer, but I can see that they must win out for the good of England. It affects not only our commerce but our navy. The sea is our wall of defense, and it will take ships to defend it. Dost remember that ancient pun that the Dutch made when Edward III ordered the gold noble to be struck with a ship design? They insolently asked why we did not have it engraved with a sheep instead. We shall yet show them," and Sir Frederick rose and paced the floor, for his anger mounted at the thought.

Lady Mathilda grew still more serious. "Knowest thou not what happens to the man who is in advance of his times?" she cautioned. "Be careful, I beg of thee, for not all men can see as far as thou canst."

"Have no fear. All will be well, and thou wouldst not have me do otherwise than as I see best. Within the year I shall have three ships, but the first shall be Johanna's. Thou shalt name it, child, and the fortune that it brings shall go into thy dower. I have this day promised thee in marriage, when thou art of age, to Sir Richard's son. However," he hastened to add as if he did not wish to linger on this event, "that is far off, and need not be thought of yet."

Lady Mathilda at this point burst into tears. Sir Frederick was astonished, and Johanna hastened to her side.

"Why, Mathilda!"

"Why, Mother!"

"'Tis nothing," said Lady Mathilda between her sobs. "I do but fear for thee, and what with the loss of the key and all, I am upset."

"Come," said Sir Frederick kindly, "we talk of too serious things. Let us go into the garden," and taking her by the arm, he led her through the wide door. Johanna followed, thinking of many things.

CHAPTER IV. DISMAS DOES NOT COME

DEEP in the fens above Boston was a small lake, landlocked at low tide, but at high tide joined by pools and streams, which met the swollen Lindis. On one of its sides was a large clump of huge willows, while on its other sides were boglands where sedges and rushes grew tall and luxuriant, and open marshes over which wild swans flew. Among these willows Tod of the Fens and his band of fenmen had built rude huts, and before them now they were gathered, cooking fish over a small bed of hot embers. Many small skiffs were drawn up at the water's edge, and leaning against the trees here and there were heavy oaken stilts.

"He cannot get back except at high tide," Tod said, as he turned the spit on which a row of good-sized salmon was fixed, "and it lacks a good hour of that. But the moon will be full to-night and I wager he will get here as he said he would. Could he but use the stilts with skill, and handle the skiff on his back, as we do, he would get here earlier."

"Could he but use the stilts! Alackaday! he is like a young heron that has no control over his legs," another of the band put in, called Heron himself, because he was the most skilled on long legs. "Have I myself not been trying to teach him, and have rescued him from the bog a many time because he does not pick the hard places, but falls on his head where the mud be the softest, and most likely to swallow him whole? 'Egad!' he says,' 'tis the soft places I would choose for such falls as I do take!' And who may this Dismas be, Master Tod?"

"Another who loves adventuring even as we do, good Heron. Have we ever asked who thou be?"

"Nay, it is true, we know not of each other except that we be a right good company, and that we do all wish to teach men what wisdom we can, and, after all, it is a merry life with all the world to fool! And who be the greatest fool this day?"

"Methinks it be this same Dismas, for has he not promised that given a week and a day, he would make all the townsfolk of Boston into as silly a set as could be found in the whole length and breadth of Merry England!" It was another of the band who spoke, a ruddy-faced, lightly built man with a comical twist to his mouth and a bald crown to his head.

"Thou art afraid, Tom True Tongue," said another. "Thou art afraid he will win his wager, and that will mean the ducking stool for thee, for thou didst boast that thou couldst fool more men in a week and a day than he in the same length of time. Come now, tell us what thou hast done!"

"That is all very well," said the one thus addressed, "but how knowest thou that we can believe his story? He will have naught to prove it, belike."

"Thinkest thou I know not when men lie." It was Tod himself who spoke. "Have ye not chosen me for master because not one of ye can tell a lie without I prove it on ye, and send ye straightway to the ducking stool!"

"Ay, ay," shouted the others. "He that can fool Tod of the Fens then shall be master!"

"But thou, Tom, who art surnamed True Tongue, thou hast forgot the many duckings thou didst have before thou didst earn that title," said Tod, laughing at the recollection he had of some of them.

"But, come now, let us all eat, for the fish is cooked to a turn. After we have eaten, we shall hear Tom's tale, and then when the moon comes, we shall take sides in a tilting match."

"Why not Tom's tale now while we do eat?"

"Ay, why not, Bat, thou salmon-eater?" answered Tom instantly. "So that thou canst have my portion of salmon no doubt. I like not to share a trencher with thee, for thou pushest naught but the bones my way."

"To the ducking stool with him, master, for he lies!"

"Nay, Bat," answered Tod good-naturedly, "that be as true a word as he has ever spoken, for I have eaten with thee more than once. But come, fetch out the bread and ale."

The men did as they were bidden without further urging, and when the meal was over, they stretched themselves on the ground at full length.

"Now, then," said Tod, "I have thy account here, Tom True Tongue, and already there be fifteen notches, a good reckoning for a week's time. 'Tis the record so far."

"And how stands Dismas's?" asked another of the band.

Tod held up a second tally. "This be his, and so far he has but five, but he has until twelve tonight, and he says there will not be room on the stick for all the notches he will have earned."

"And what think ye he is up to?" asked Tom True Tongue curiously. "Here has he gone each day, and when afternoon comes, back he hies with the greatest collection of clothes I have ever seen, and where think ye that he gets them? To-day he set off in a minstrel's garb as gay as ye please, and with as big a bundle under his arm as if he were going to play the part of my Lord Bishop of Canterbury. 'Twas late when he left, for he spent the day playing a harp and practicing a song, which he seems to be trying to recall. 'Twas something about a noble Moringer. He will have to sing it to us when he has it well in hand."

"Mayhap he would be caught and hung for a thief, if I had not shown him the trick of the Lindis whereby ye can leave your skiff in the rushes well above the bridge, and pick it up at high tide on the town side near Wormgate. It would not be so easy for him, belike, if he did not have that means of getting away. I have never known it to fail."

"Nor I either," said another fenman. "At full of the tide thou canst climb the wall, drop over on the ditch side, and below is thy skiff waiting as if guided there by some boatman."

"'Tis easy enough to see that it is caught in the current at full tide and swept down. Just this side of the bridge a cross current hits it and carries it in."

"Ay, truly, but it is only at spring tide that it works that way, and as I said, he is in luck, or some of the townsfolk would catch him at his deviltry."

"How is it that he has collected his disguises?"

"By fair means enough, and for each of them have I given him a notch, for he says there be five fools who have given up their gowns to him so long as they thereby fatten their wallets, and he has proof enough of that!"

"Ay, truly, for has he not been mimicking around here, first as one and then as another, till I myself have almost been fooled as to whether he be himself or some one else?"

"Ay, and that is why I would know whether 'tis himself or some one else that we do know. Belike he does think to fool us all. Thou hadst best look out, Master Tod, or thou wilt no longer be master here."

"Ay," answered Tod, "but if ever he comes to stating that he is other than I know him to be, then shall ye see. Never fear that his tally shall be notched for me."

"Thou dost know him then?"

"I did know him the moment I did lay mine eyes upon him, but enough of this! Come, Tom True Tongue, tell us what thou hast been up to!"

"Not much this day, forsooth," began Tom True Tongue. "This morning I set out for Wickham Ford, and there sat I dreaming under a tree with my rod and line beside me. The sun was warm, and the flies did buzz delightfully so that I dozed. When I awoke, the sun was high, and I took out my slice of bread and my wedge of cheese, and thought to eat my morning meal. Coming along the road I saw a gay company of courtiers, and they be laughing and talking, and their mounts glistened in the sun with the silver trappings that they bore. They themselves were finely clad with hats and plumes, and dagged sleeves to their tunics, and the long toes of their shoes hanging far out of their stirrups. Then did I pretend to be asleep.

"'Ho! ho, there!' called the foremost one, who seemed to be the gayest of them all, 'a pest upon thee for sleeping there when good men do need thee to guide them! Is there a benighted town called Boston lost somewhere in these fens? If thou canst put us on the right road thereto, I'll say thou art a better man than thou lookest to be.'

"'Ay, thou hast the look of a rogue! But we'll promise not to set the hue and cry after thee, if so thou set us straight,' said another.

"With that they came plunging through the ford, and I sat up, and blinked, and slapped the air as if a gnat disturbed me. Then turned I over on the other side and thought to sleep again.

"'How now, art deaf?' and the leader urged his horse as if to run me over.

"'Alack,' quoth I, 'methought I dreamed, and dreaming was I in an assembly of great and noble courtiers, and waking do I see nothing but the blue sky overhead and the green trees waving.'

"'Then dream again, fool,' vouchsafed another, 'and tell these same dream courtiers the way to Boston town, for we have not the time to give to thy dreaming and thy waking.'

"'So be it,' I answered, 'since they wish to go to Boston town so must they come out of my dream, for in it they do not go to Boston town but to the worst bog-hole that there be in the whole of this great stretch of fens. To get there needs must they follow this road, until at the next turning they bear to the right and come out upon an oozy stretch.'

"'Heaven protect us from any oozy stretches, for well do I know that our horses would go in up to their ears,' exclaimed another. 'If this road leads to the worst bog-hole in the fens, then must we go the way we have come and seek some other way.'

"With that they wheeled their horses and splashed back through the ford, and as they went, I heard them say something about the madcap Prince Hal, at which they all burst into loud laughter.

"After they left, I continued my eating. Then did I fish. Along toward the middle of the afternoon I heard galloping, and back over the road came the cavalcade. They were not as gay this time, for they were splashed with mud from much riding. I concealed myself in an alder thicket.

"'Alack!' quoth one, 'here we be but at the same spot that we gained this morning, but well do I know now that Boston does not lie far from here. It was that dreaming fool that did set us wrong.'

"'Ay, we have him to thank for a fine day's splashing, and had we but time I would hunt him down and give him a good sound beating that might wake him from his dreaming.'

"With that they passed from sight, and I doubt not that they reached Bargate within a short space, but they do know more than they did ere I spoke to them, for they must be well acquainted with the fens, forsooth."

"And that be our motto indeed – to leave men wiser than we find them, so I suppose thou must even have more notches on thy tally," said Tod when Tom's tale came to an end, and the fenmen continued to laugh loud and long as they always did at Tom True Tongue's drollery.

"Give me but five, for there were but five in the party, but if one of them was the madcap prince himself it seems as if it ought to count higher than anything Dismas can do!"

"Ay, ay," agreed the band in unison.

"So be it," answered Tod, "but wait until we hear from Dismas ere we decide! Now do ye, Wat and Perkin, divide us into two sides, for the moon is up, and we must be at our tilting."

With that the men sprang up, and under Wat's and Perkin's directions, six skiffs were pushed off, two men in each skiff. One plied the oars and the other stood with a rough wooden shield and a wooden lance well up in the bow. First they rowed a good distance in opposite directions, then separating to allow for a good sweep of oars, they turned, and with strong and swift strokes of the oarsmen, they bore down upon each other.

The moon was well up and turned the willows on the water's edge to a soft silver. The frogs filled the air with their steady drumming, and a light mist rose from the marshes and hung over the reeds and rushes.

The contestants closed in on each other, and there was the sound of lance striking shield as the boats passed close.

"How now!" cried Tod, as he made a mighty thrust at his opponent, "canst thou, good Cedric, parry that blow and keep thy balance?"

"Ay," answered Cedric, "that can I, but thy lance is of stout oak or it would be splintered by this good shield of mine!"

"Back at him, ere he can turn!" shouted Tod to his oarsman, "and we will send him to the fishes!"

Both boats turned swiftly, and again came the crash of lances, but though the boats tipped dangerously, neither Tod nor Cedric showed any unsteadiness in his bearing.

Off to the right of them came a loud splash and cry. "Bat is overboard and he sat down right heavily," cried Tom True Tongue. "'Twill be some time before he comes up, for he is no swan's feather."

Up came Bat, puffing and splashing. His boatman rescued him and his shield, but his lance was broken in two.

"'Twas my lance that failed me!" he sputtered, as he climbed clumsily into his boat, "but the water be cold enough to freeze a frog," and he began to blow harder and to beat the air with his arms.

"Keep thy drippings to thyself or I will send thee overboard again!" cautioned his boat companion.

"Well, then, back to the shore with me ere I do freeze!" grumbled Bat.

Meanwhile on the other side of Tod and Cedric there was more splashing and shouting, for Heron was overboard and Perkin gloating over him.

"Thou canst not succeed at everything. If thou wilt outstrip us all on stilts, thou must pay for it by taking thy dousing in good part," said Perkin.

"Ay," answered Heron between gasps, "I would liefer take my dousing in good clear water than in the green slime I saw thee in the other day."

Tod and Cedric were both breathing heavily, for they had been hard at it all this time, parrying, thrusting, and balancing themselves with great skill.

"Hast had enough or wilt thou on to the finish?" asked Tod.

"If thou are content, I would say that I am warm and comfortable now, and am loath to set my teeth to chattering," answered Cedric.

"I am not afraid of that," answered Tod, "for I do not intend to go in this night, and I am loath to send thee in, for thou art a good man at tilting, and thou dost parry and thrust with strength and skill."

"Ay," answered Perkin and Wat together, "and that be the reason we set him against thee!"

"Any other of us would have been blowing bubbles in the water after thy second thrust," said another of the band, "and that thou knowest, Master Tod."

"Let us to the shore then," quoth Tod, "for it is well on toward midnight."

"The tide has turned," called Tom True Tongue, "and Dismas has not come."

"Mayhap he be sitting this moment at the hut awaiting our return."

"He is not here," called Bat from the shore, as all the boats came in.

"Then have I won the wager!" announced Tom True Tongue, "and I would have thee know that when he does return, to the ducking stool he goes, and 'twill do my heart good to see him go under, for I do not like the way he thinks to join our band and beat us at our own sport all in a fortnight's time."

"Mayhap we shall never set eyes on him again. What reason have we to think that he will come back for his ducking? Wouldst thou thyself return but for a ducking, Tom True Tongue?"

"Perhaps he will not return for his ducking, but didst think I would let him go as easily as that? Think ye he will return for this?" and Tom True Tongue drew from his breast a silver badge. The band drew around as he held it in his palm in the clear moonlight.

"'Tis three ostrich feathers encircled by a crown," said Tom True Tongue, "and know ye whose badge is that?"

Each fenman looked at it in turn, and shook his head. Tod only withdrew, shaking inwardly with laughter.

"When he gave it to me," continued Tom True Tongue, "he did say that he would return for it, or else that with it I would have no trouble in tracing him down."

"Then thou must trace him down," called Tod, "for since he has not come by this time, I do fear that he will not come."

CHAPTER V.
THE COFFER KEYS

IT was market day in Boston. Since daybreak and the opening of the town gates, peasants had been streaming in from the surrounding countryside with heavily laden pack horses bearing vegetables, milk, poultry, butter and eggs, and sacks of grain. Every one was about some task or other, for the stalls had to be set up around the market place in the shadow of St. Botolph's church from which even now people were coming from early mass. Town officials were collecting rent on the stalls already taken up, and apprentice boys were hurrying hither and yon at the excited bidding of their masters.

Johanna, accompanied by Caroline who carried a large flat basket for purchases, was among the early arrivals at the market, for it was well to be early if one wished the best of the wares. However, they were not as early as Dame Pinchbeck, whose loud voice could be heard above the general bustle and confusion, her broad back and still broader front with its full folds of gown gathered about her waist, assuring her a goodly space before any stall. She had been the first to answer the ringing of the market bell that announced the opening for trade.

"Come, Caroline," said Johanna, "if we would have the full fun of market day, we must be within hearing of Dame Pinchbeck." They crossed the square to the foot of the market cross and joined Dame Pinchbeck before the butcher's booth.

"Good day, Dame Pinchbeck," said Johanna, but Dame Pinchbeck had no breath for common words.

"I was but telling this knave of a butcher, and thy good father would agree with me, I doubt not, that I like not the way he throws out his odds and ends of hog so that I must even hold my nose as I come out mine own alley, and continue to hold it until I gain the next, all the time picking my way lest I slip on the grease. Dost think I will buy his hog? Not I. I shall buy from yonder butcher, for he befouls some other alley than mine. Come, let's purchase our greens before there is naught left but the weeds that come with them!" From the vegetable stall, their baskets well laden, they were headed for the baker's stall where Dame Pinchbeck was planning to express her mind freely in regard

DAME PINCHBECK.

to a light loaf she believed she had been given the last time she had purchased, when an exciting, but not altogether unusual, event took place.

Dame Pinchbeck was in the lead and had but gained the most open part of the square when a flock of sheep on the way to the mart yard on the further side of the town burst in from a side street, followed by a harassed sheep dog and a howling shepherd. In another moment the place was filled with sheep, frightened creatures that piled up on each other, first against one stall, and then from that to another, where the shopkeepers and townsfolk together tried to save the trestle tables from collapse. Dame Pinchbeck was caught in the tide of oncoming sheep. First this way and then that was she hurried, and at no time was she given a chance to emerge, for always did she appear to form the center of the moving mass. Her vegetables were scattered, and with her empty basket she was adding to the confusion and her own implication in it, for, with both hands gripping its edge, she was belaboring the nearest sheep as the others closed in around her. At last the frantic sheep dog succeeded in heading them into an outlet, and Dame Pinchbeck was left alone in a state of great bewilderment.

It was not until their wares were safe that the townsfolk had time to laugh, but then such a wave of mirth swept through the market place that even the staid old burgesses held their sides and the apprentice boys rolled on the ground.

"She will never get her breath back to scold again!" said the butcher who had just received his share of her scolding.

"Alackaday!" laughed his apprentice, "she was skipping as gayly as a young maid round a Maypole!"

Johanna and Caroline hurried to her side, but Dame Pinchbeck had already recovered and had set about collecting what she could of the young cabbages she had purchased. Many of them had been trampled, but she assured Johanna they were no worse than many a peasant would like to sell her for the best price. "In these days thou must keep thine eyes open if thou wouldst not be cheated," she went on. "As I was saying before I got interrupted, if thou dost not prod under the bread trough while thy dough is being mixed, as like as not a rascal of an apprentice is set there to pull the dough away from underneath while thou countest full measures being poured in at the top. The world is full of rascals, but there be but few that get the best of Dame Pinchbeck!" She poked her head around a draper's booth gay with its scarlet and green cloth, where a young apprentice sat swinging his legs and chanting, "What do ye lack? What do ye lack?"

"Art trying to be a linnet?" inquired Dame Pinchbeck with great scorn in her voice. "But I doubt not if I should buy of thee, I would lack a good half ell of my measure, for thy fat thumb would gain at least two inches on each turn of the stick. What askest thou for that bit of bright embroidery?"

"Two farthing the ell," was the quick answer of the apprentice, "and I wager thou couldst not get a bit as fine as that anywhere else. It would look well on thy goodman's gown, for I hear he is alderman these five months past."

"Out upon thee for a rascal," answered Dame Pinchbeck. "Two farthing the ell! Did I not get finer stuff than that from a chapman last week? And what thinkest thou that I gave him? Naught but a handful of old iron, as I live, and I left with five ells of the trimming, and good lengths at that."

It was now time for the market to be opened for traders, for the custom was that the townsfolk should have the first opportunity to buy the necessaries, as butter, eggs, and poultry, before the traders bought up the supply. Johanna and Caroline had left Dame Pinchbeck and had finished their purchases before the second bell rang, and the market place became thronged with traders from far and near and with strangers of high rank and low.

As they passed by the tavern, Johanna noticed a group of men, drinking together at the broad table before the door.

"They be Easterlings," said Johanna to Caroline, as they hurried past, "and I like not their looks. Didst notice how coarse and red their faces were, and large-featured?"

"Ay, mistress," answered Caroline, "they have not the clear, honest look of Englishmen."

"If one can believe Dame Pinchbeck," laughed Johanna, "there be no such thing as honesty in Englishmen either. Didst ever see a funnier sight than she floundering in a sea of sheep, her kerchief acting like a sail, while she plied her basket as madly as a boatman does his oar?" and Johanna laughed out merrily at the remembrance of the incident.

As her clear laugh reached the men at the table, one of them turned and followed her with his eyes.

"Herr Tilney's daughter, nicht wahr?" he asked in a deep guttural voice, and went on in German: "Speak of the Devil, and his daughter passes!" From which it appears that Sir Frederick had been the subject of conversation.

"Speaking of the Devil himself," broke in another, and he, too, spoke in

German, "dost know the funny legend that these simpletons of Boston believe? It seems that there is always a gust of wind circulating at the foot of yonder tower," and he pointed across to St. Botolph's steeple. "It can be felt in the daytime, but at night it is worse. No good Boston folk will venture there after the sun goes down, and what think ye it is? It is the Devil himself blowing!" and the speaker burst into a loud guffaw, and brought his fist down sharply on the table.

"What makes them think so?" asked another curiously.

"Why, the story goes that their good saint himself, when he was puffed with pride with the good works that he had accomplished, was strolling there one evening, and the Devil appeared before him. Then did he know that the pride in him was but the Devil tempting him, and he fought with him forthwith. Such was the strength with which he grappled with him, that the poor Devil needs must puff and blow, and he puffs and he blows to this day, and will as long as St. Botolph's steeple stands, for the Devil hopes to bring it down in revenge for his thrashing."

"A good tale," said the one who first spoke, "and is it true no townsman will go there after sundown?"

"True as I live, and I'll pay for the ale if the innkeeper does not back me up."

"I'll believe thee, for well do I know thou wouldst not offer to do that without thou wert sure of thy ground. I have never known thee to throw thy money to the wind, even be it such a one as be raised by the Devil's own blowing!"

"Come now, Ranolf," said the other, "thou art in a pretty temper, and all because Herr Tilney caught thee trying to smuggle wool through. 'Tis a wonder he did not have thee put in the pillory so that all the townsfolk could shower thee with rotten eggs. All he did was to take from thee a few of thine ill-gotten gains."

"He will repent the doing of that before I get through," was the gruff response.

"Hast heard," broke in another, "that he is going into the carrying trade himself? He has one ship already under way and a second one he thinks to purchase from a Lynn merchant, the one who sailed in the other day?"

"Let him! Dost think these simple Englishmen can ever compete with us on the high seas? Pfaff! They are like the silly sheep they raise and are only fit for shearing. But what thinkest thou of this?" and the one they called Ranolf threw a glance around to see who might be near enough to hear, and then leaning far over the table, he beckoned the others to draw close, and he spoke in low tones.

* * * * * * * * * * *

Immediately after the close of the market, the bailiff and the town council met in the Guild Hall, for it was necessary to check the collections of the town officials, and open the town coffer to receive them.

Hugh Witham, High Bailiff, sat at the end of the huge table, covered with a green baize cloth, and around him were gathered the councilmen, among them Sir Frederick Tilney.

"My Lord Bailiff, before we can go very far with the business of the day," began Sir Frederick, "I must announce a loss which has lately occurred to me. My key to the town coffer was taken from my house yesterday." The bailiff's face and the faces of three other men went white. "The loss of one key could not endanger the treasure, so that – " But here Sir Frederick was interrupted.

"I thought the same," stammered Hugh Witham in great agitation, "for my key also is missing. How is it with thee, William Spayne, and thee, Roger Pinchbeck, and thee, Alan Marflete?"

One look at the faces of the councilmen thus called upon was sufficient for the assembled company to realize that they, too, were in the same predicament, and a general burst of dismay and consternation followed.

"The coffer has been robbed," announced the bailiff in a weak voice, "and according to the last accounting it contained two hundred marks!"

"Two hundred marks!"

"We be ruined indeed!"

"Come now!" It was Sir Frederick who was the first to regain his composure. "The robbers must be found. Each one must tell how it was that his key was taken. As for me it was in this wise," and he related the account given him by Lady Mathilda of the apprentice. When he had finished, he turned to Roger Pinchbeck. "Thou next, Roger Pinchbeck."

Roger Pinchbeck was a large man with a round jovial face, which just now did not look as jovial as was its wont.

"Know then I do not tell my good wife everything I know for fear it may go farther, for she has a tongue. I left the key in my house without telling her it was of special value. She threw it in with a handful of iron which a chapman asked in exchange for some trinket she fancied, and I have not dared tell her yet what it is he has done, for she will berate me soundly, and say I was but a noddy not to give it into her keeping!"

A smile passed over the faces of the other councilmen, but the bailiff spoke sharply. "This is no time for smiling," he said. "I cannot say how it was that I lost my key, and yet I do feel 'twas taken last night when I did stand but for a short space listening to a minstrel at the 'Golden Fleece.' Afterward when I reached home it was missing from my wallet. I went back thinking I did but drop it, but I could not find it anywhere. It is the minstrel I suspect, for he did jostle against me as he went the rounds, collecting his small fees."

"Then there be four in league," broke in William Spayne, who was a small man with rather a large head, surmounted with a flat cap and a long liripipe, "for I am sure mine must have fallen into a peasant's sack when I was testing it to the bottom to see that all be fair. 'Twas not all fair, but full of husks and dust, so I sent him on his way. After he was gone, I missed the key which I wore around my neck. That was a week ago yesterday."

"And what hast thou to say for thyself, Alan Marflete?" demanded the bailiff. "It is certain that we all be fools at the mercy of some band of rogues."

"I know not who made the fool of me," answered Marflete, getting redder than the red gown that he wore. "I am a religious man, and give my money to the church as ye all know, and far be it from me to suspect a friar who held converse with me last evening, but know ye that he did bid me close my eyes and pray with him a space, the which I did. Then he passed on around the Blackfriars convent, and I homeward in deep thought. Ere I reached my door I missed the key from my belt, and retraced my steps, even as our bailiff did, but there was no friar to be seen, only the minstrel whom we all heard sing not many minutes later."

There was several minutes' silence, for each pondered in wonderment at the variety of the tales that had been called forth. Then Hugh Witham spoke. "Summon Simon Gough, and we shall see if he can throw any light on this queer business. Mayhap he has noticed some of these same rogues coming or going past his gate."

Not long after Simon Gough stood before them, wondering wherefore he had been summoned.

"Hast seen any suspicious people going over thy bridge this week past, Simon?" asked Sir Frederick.

"Ay, Sire, the world be full of rogues!" answered Simon with assurity.

"Didst mark any leave the town to-day in company, a motley company forsooth, a minstrel, a friar, a peasant, a chapman, and an apprentice lad?"

For a second, light broke over Simon's countenance, but he answered, "Nay, Sire. I have seen no such company."

"Hast seen any of these separately leaving town?" asked the bailiff. "Thou didst look but now as if thou didst have some idea, forsooth."

"Nay, your Honor, it is not separately they went."

"We shall arrive at naught. Thou mayest return to thy duty, Simon." Whereupon Simon withdrew, stepping as lightly as his heavy clogs allowed.

"The best thing we can do," announced the bailiff, "is to make the loss known to the townsfolk. With every one on the watch it may not be too late to find the thieves."

As Simon returned to his gatehouse he slapped his pouch, and then pushed back his hood, and scratched his head.

"Ay," he thought, "I knew there was some trouble brewing, but what good would it do them to know that I have seen him? He be gone by this time, and it is not every one would have thought to have left Simon Gough with two good nobles!"

CHAPTER VI. ENTER LORD ARUNDEL

GREAT was the sensation in Boston when the news was spread that the keys to the town coffer had been taken, and tongues other than Dame Pinchbeck's were busy the next morning. The story told by each of the town officers who had suffered the loss was stretched like the cloth that belonged to the fuller who wished to gain an ell or more in length, or to make up the requirement in breadth of two ells within the list.

"Knowest thou," screamed Dame Pinchbeck from the alley to her neighbor, Dame Skilton, who was at her loom, "that 'twas a bold-faced thief of a minstrel who set upon our good bailiff – set upon him and knocked him senseless on the way to his home the night before last. The poor man's head is still sore from the blow, and belike he will never be himself again. Tis likely enough we shall all be knocked about and robbed."

"Thou didst not have any ill effects from thy encounter with the chapman, didst thou?" called back Dame Skilton, above the bang of the comb and the clank of the treadle.

"Nay, not I," answered Dame Pinchbeck. "Thou knowest the saying:'

Adam and Eve and Pinchbeck
Went down to the river to bathe,
Adam and Eve got drownded,
And who dost think got saved?

He addressed me fair enough, and a fine-looking fellow was he, but tall. He was a young giant, for he must have had six feet."

"Dost say that he had six feet? Alackaday! I have never heard of such a likelihood! And what did he do with them all? If he were not a thief, I should like to have him to run my loom, for six feet would certainly be useful."

"Ha! ha!" laughed Dame Pinchbeck. "Thou art always poking fun at me. But as I was saying, he spoke me fair, and now, I ask thee, had not the key been of value, wouldst thou not say I had struck a good bargain? Thou didst see the embroidery that I did take. He had but a few trinkets in his pack, for he said his day had been fine, and the goodwives of Boston did know what they were about, for they bought wisely and well."

Dame Pinchbeck had crossed the cobbled lane by this time, and was leaning against the doorway, and watching Dame Skilton as she deftly tossed the shuttle back and forth.

"My goodman says," Dame Skilton continued, "that there be whispers about that Sir Frederick Tilney knows more about this robbing of the coffer than they like to think of his knowing. 'Twas he that was the first to break the news, and now does he suggest that the two hundred marks be made up by the five officers in fault. 'Twill mean forty marks apiece, and that be a great sum."

Dame Pinchbeck gasped, and then sat down heavily on the bench within the door.

"I had not heard that," she declared, leaning forward in astonishment and the words coming out with breathless pauses between. "And prithee, how is my goodman to meet that, I ask thee? 'Tis well enough for Sir Frederick, but how about us poor folk?"

"Ay, that is what they say, and though everybody knows the reputation of the Tilney family, still the whisper goes about that mayhap forty marks from two hundred marks leaves the balance a good one, and worth the loss of the forty marks."

"Dost mean by that that Sir Frederick would have the one hundred and sixty marks?" gasped Dame Pinchbeck.

"I did not say so," answered Dame Skilton cautiously. "I did but repeat what I have heard rumored. There is other talk about Sir Frederick being suddenly taken with the idea of shipbuilding, and forsaking the wool trade, and what not. I know not what it means or where it all may lead, but I be one of those who care not who forsakes the wool trade. It is as much as we can do to get wool for our own weaving, so set are the wool merchants to send our English wool abroad. This place be full of wool as thou knowest, and yet does my goodman have to work hard to get enough to keep our two looms going."

Dame Pinchbeck's thoughts were on other things than this common complaint of the English weaver of this time, for there were the forty marks Pinchbeck might have to hand over, and although he did indeed have a full leathern bag carefully hidden away, still it would be lightened almost entirely by the loss of such a sum.

Meanwhile in the "Golden Fleece" there was a scene in progress that we must indeed look in on, rather than delay longer at this gossiping.

"How now, thou madcap Hal, here do we come upon thee playing the minstrel and warbling thy songs to the dull-witted townsfolk of Boston? Hast never heard that Boston ears be stuffed with wool?"

The speaker was an elegantly dressed nobleman with a clear-cut face and arched brow. He wore an ermine-trimmed scarlet houppelande, and his carefully dressed locks reached to his shoulders and curled at the nape of his neck. The toes of his shoes were fastened by long gold chains to his knees, and across his shoulder was a baldrick, which was hung with small bells.

"Come now, tell us what thou hast been up to this fortnight past." And he waved his hand to include the group of four other noblemen who were seated by the window and who were dividing their attention between some small talk of their own and what the others were saying.

The person thus addressed, who was in reality none other than Henry of Monmouth, Prince of Wales, stood before the speaker in an attitude of defiance. "How now, my lord of Arundel, since when hast thou taken upon thyself to be my guardian? Can I not disport myself as I would without giving thee an accounting? Rather do thou tell me what thou and thy fine retainers are doing here."

"We have been dispatched from Castle Bolingbroke to search thee out. We thought to find thee here, perchance, knowing thy fondness for the haunts of men, but we did not think to spend one day splashing through the fens and ruining our clothes, and another ere in this dull town, and then to have nothing for our trouble but dark looks from thee! And here have I loaned thee my second best attire that thou mightest discard that minstrel garb of thine, and for that even do I get no thanks."

"Ay, thou shouldst indeed thank him for that," called a young man from across the room, "for he did take great pains in bringing it hither, for such is his conceit that he loathes to wear the same attire two days in succession."

"And yet for thee I am wearing this three days," said Lord Arundel, flicking a speck from his baldrick and setting the silver bells to tinkling.

"Thou needst not have gone against thy custom, for I should have been willing to take that one thou didst wear upon thy arrival, and thou couldst have had this," said Prince Henry, whereupon there was loud laughter from the others. "Didst not hear him say that was his second best? It is his best that he does wear."

"I thought so," answered Prince Henry grimly, "but I do thank thee for it just the same, and more, that thou didst have the good sense to keep silent when thou didst discover me the other night. But now what is the message that thou dost bring? Out with it, and then leave me in peace."

"We cannot leave thee, for to bring thee back with us was the substance of our message."

The Prince was silent for a short time, and then his face lightened, and he broke into laughter.

"That being the case," he said, "then thou must stay behind to finish up my business."

"And what might that be?" asked Lord Arundel dubiously. "There is certainly something mysterious about it, for thou didst naught but hush us up when we came upon thee and bid us wait until now before we spoke with thee. What hast thou been about?"

"Know then, if it be any satisfaction to thee, that I did not do as I wished, for thy coming did upset my plans. However, be that as it may, thanks to these fine clothes thou gavest me, I can now lean further on thy goodness and return to Bolingbroke on thy horse."

"And I?" questioned Lord Arundel, raising his eyebrows,

"I will explain to thee outside the hearing of these other gentlemen." The Prince and Lord Arundel withdrew to the end of the room where the small diamond-paned lattice window looked out on to the market place, where townsfolk were lingering in groups, gesticulating, calling back and forth, and breaking away from one group to join another.

"There is something astir here in this town. See how excited they be below," said Lord Arundel, poking his aristocratic head out. "I was awakened early this morning by the clanging of the bell, and it seems a pity that they could not do it at a more seasonable hour than just as the sun appears and when their betters would be sleeping."

"'Tis nothing that concerns thee," answered Prince Henry lightly, "for it is some affair of the town council apparently. But I must be off, so listen to what I have to say. I made a light wager with a fenman whom I would have thee seek out for me. Tell him I sent thee to take the payment which he would give me. Wilt do this for me?"

"And what will the payment be?" asked Lord Arundel.

"'Twill be the price of the fine clothes thou dost wear," and a twinkle came into Prince Henry's eye. "That much I promise thee for undertaking this."

"Thou meanest that?" asked Lord Arundel eagerly. "I will indeed do as thou sayest if thereby I do acquire another fine attire. Dost know the styles are changing fast, and I would drop this high-collared houppelande with its long skirt and cut the skirt to the knees with neat dags," and in his burst of enthusiasm, Lord Arundel fell to gesticulating and twirling about. "The sleeves I'd drop to here," he continued, designating a length at least a foot greater than the ones he was then wearing, "and with buttons to the waist, and belted in, how thinkest thou it would look?"

Prince Henry was overcome with quiet mirth. "I know naught about fashions," he managed to vouchsafe, "nor did I think to start thy tongue going at such a rate, but listen to what thou must do, if thou wouldst bring about this new creation," and Prince Henry explained how he must take a certain skiff then beached without the town and seek out the inland lake and the haunt of Tod of the Fens. "If thou start out this noon at high tide, thou canst not get astray, and when thou dost find the hut, wait there until Tod or Tom True Tongue appear. 'Tis with the latter that the business is. Then they will guide thee to Horncastle where thy horse will be sent for thee."

"Art sure thou art not sending me to a den of thieves?"

"As sure as I am that I am here before thee. I am sending thee to as honest and upright a band of men as there be anywhere in England. On this I pledge my honor."

"'Tis not to my liking," said Lord Arundel, "but then if I am to have another attire, it will not matter so much if this gets a bit of hard wear. What am I to say to this Tod of the Fens or this Tom Tongue Tie?"

"Say just these words that I now tell thee. 'Dismas was delayed, and could not keep the tryst. I am come at his bidding to take the payment Tom True Tongue would give, for which thou must notch Dismas's tally once more.' Remember I am known only as Dismas."

"Thou art known only as Dismas, and he is known only as Tom Tongue Tie, and between the two of ye I may be known only as food for kites! Egad! I may be robbed and tied up to a tree!"

"Nay, nay," expostulated Prince Henry, "'tis not so! I swear it! Repeat then the message and get thee gone!"

Lord Arundel repeated the words after the prince, although he still showed signs of doubt and mistrust of the whole undertaking. Shortly after, Prince Henry left Boston, and be it said for him that the froth which he stirred up did not settle for a long time after his going. Riding away to Bolingbroke to turn his fickle attention to the king's business, this prince who was such a strange mixture of mischief and gravity left behind him a complicated situation which took curious twists and turns before he again appeared to take a part in it. In his various disguises he had secured the keys to the town coffer just as the town officers had related. Then was he interrupted by the appearance of the party from Bolingbroke and prevented from returning to the fens in time to win his wager with Tom True Tongue. Great as his disappointment was not to relate his story of having fooled the whole town of Boston into believing the coffer was robbed, and to see the droll Tom True Tongue squirming and howling on the ducking stool, still there was some satisfaction in the way things were working out. He had decided that St. Botolph alone could be trusted with the keys to the town coffer and he left them concealed in a cornice at the foot of the steeple. The whole situation was thus in the good saint's hands, and it would be for him to assist his townspeople as he saw fit. Then there was the fine Lord Arundel even then on his way to the fens to take Dismas's place at the ducking stool.

Prince Henry burst out into a sudden laugh as he pictured Lord Arundel in the fens. So sudden and so loud was his outburst that the other horsemen turned to look at him in astonishment, and his own horse shied under him. If Tod of the Fens could have heard him, he would have thought that his pupil had learned the art of laughter well in his fortnight and a day.

"Forsooth!" he was thinking, "that ducking will indeed be the price of the fine clothes he is wearing! Ha! ha! ha!" And this time more than one horse started up at the roar, and the whole cavalcade broke into a lively gallop.

PRINCE HENRY HAD SECURED THE KEYS.

CHAPTER VII. MORE ABOUT THE MERCHANT ADVENTURERS

SIR FREDERICK TILNEY was greatly disturbed, and Lady Mathilda's forebodings were in a measure fulfilled. Things seemed to be crowding in on Sir Frederick. Here was he pledged to Sir Richard Branche to have two ships to join the fleet which should set out before midsummer to attend the great fair at Novgorod. One of these he must build and man, and the other he was buying equipped from Sir Richard for the large sum of three hundred marks. The former would cost him somewhat more. On top of this had come the robbing of the town coffer and his responsibility in connection with it. Then, too, there was a disturbing event with a certain Easterling named Ranolf, whose glowering looks he had to encounter each day as he came and went about his business. Lady Mathilda was not able to give him much advice, and an unaccountable coolness seemed to have sprung up in the attitude of many of his fellow townsmen, so that it was to Johanna that Sir Frederick turned, for young as she was, there was a depth of understanding and a courage in her which often helped him.

They sat this afternoon in the little arbor overlooking the pond. The swans were swimming around, with heads and long necks appearing and disappearing under the water. Close beside the arbor were little beds of daffodils and violets, and the fragrance of the latter filled the air.

"Dost know what I have decided to call my ship, father?" Johanna was asking.

"I think I shall call her the 'White Swan of Boston'!"

"So?" queried her father absently.

"Ay," pursued Johanna, "dost not like the name? It will be after that large swan of ours, for it is such a fine bird, and lucky it is, too. I feel sure a ship named after it would bring us good fortune."

Still her father seemed so preoccupied that Johanna was silent for a while. Sir Frederick was the next to speak.

"Mayhap I have been unwise," he mused half to himself and half to Johanna. "The Merchant Adventurers are but young and have only just received their charter from the king. They have taken up residence in Holland, Brabant, Zeeland, and Flanders. Since we have moved the staple town from Bruges to Calais, they have taken that for their mart town. They claim an ancient origin in the Brotherhood of St. Thomas à Becket of Canterbury, the special privileges of which were obtained from the Duke of Brabant two hundred years ago. They are concerned with the importing of English-made cloth into the cities and lands wherein they are planted. Any one paying the fee of an old noble may consort and trade with them. It well may be that I am moving in advance of my times, but it seems as if my eyes had been opened to a vision. It may not come in my lifetime, but it will come. These Merchant Adventurers will bring honor and renown to England."

Johanna listened, her eyes gleaming and her face flushed, and although it did not come in Sir Frederick's time or Johanna's either, the English Merchant Adventurers were indeed the forerunners of the great chartered companies. They were private citizens working under the sanction of the king, whereby they combined with one another to serve at once their own interests and those of their country. It was these companies that made the building of the empire possible. Their charters enabled them as Englishmen sojourning in foreign parts to govern themselves. Exactly two hundred years later the charter given to the Virginia Company can almost be said to have been modeled on the one of which Sir Frederick spoke as having just been granted to the Merchant Adventurers. In this way these early Merchant Adventurers were the forerunners of the founders of the English colonies in America.

"The wool trade is doomed, and is it not better to leave a sinking ship when the way is clear?"

"Thou canst still be Merchant of the Staple, canst thou not?" asked Johanna.

"Ay, but it will bring confusion which it will be hard for people to understand, and the time will come when there will be an open break."

"Then thou canst break away from the staple and all will be well," said Johanna calmly.

"We shall see! We shall see!" said Sir Frederick, "and soon thou canst come with me and see the building of thy ship. The keel is laid, and it will not be long before she will have her mast set and be ready for thy pennon."

"And what dost thou really think of the name I have chosen, the 'White Swan of Boston'?"

"It will do well enough if thou thinkest the three griffins of our coat of arms will not take offense!"

Johanna laughed. "With their lion bodies and eagle wings they will but give the 'White Swan' courage and swiftness."

"So be it then!" said Sir Frederick, pleased at her quick reply.

With these words he left Johanna, and she, still lingering beside the pond, thought further of what her father had been saying.

"Merchant Adventurers," she murmured beneath her breath. "Truly, it is a fine-sounding title. Brother Stephen, who has taught me so carefully to read and write, has taught me also of other lands where he has traveled as a pilgrim. I'll go to him now, and hear what more he has to tell."

Johanna passed out into the alley, and following a footpath which led beside a quiet stream and a sheep-fold, she skirted the center of the town and entered the enclosure of the Blackfriars convent from the rear. It was the time when she was sure to find Brother Stephen in the little garden, where she knew it was permissible for her to seek him out.

Over the close-clipped hedge she could see his bent back even now, his ruddy face, and his bald head with its fringe of hair.

"Brother Stephen," began Johanna as she sank down on the turf-covered seat not far from him, "wilt tell me again about St. Hugh of Lincoln?"

Brother Stephen looked up and smiled.

"Art thou here, Johanna? I was but thinking of thee, for these straight young shoots that are about to break out into bright gay daffodils do remind me of thee. They love the wind and sun even as thou dost."

"And they, too, are confined in a little enclosure and can but dream of things beyond," sighed Johanna.

"Ay," answered Brother Stephen, "but remember that they look straight up to Heaven, and does he who can see Heaven care that he cannot see the things of the Earth?"

Brother Stephen dropped the spade with which he had been loosening the earth in the flower beds, and getting down on his knees, he carefully worked around the roots of the young plants with his hands. Johanna liked to watch his serene face as he cared for the flowers he loved so dearly.

"Dear Brother Stephen, thou knowest I am not good as thou art, but I am not so bad that I am not grateful for thy teaching."

Then as the shadows deepened around the Gothic walls of the convent with its lofty windows stained with lovely colors, Brother Stephen told her of St. Hugh. In a picturesque valley of France watered by the river Isere and surrounded by hills covered with scattered ruins, there was a castle in which dwelt a family whose armorial bearings bore proof of its noble origin. This was the castle of Avalon, and here was born Hugh of Avalon, later to be known as St. Hugh of Lincoln. Far off on the distant horizon from his home stood the great walls of rock which hid from the world the monastery of Grande Chartreuse. In this solitary place, surrounded by dense forests and roaring torrents, Hugh spent his young manhood in prayer and fasting. Then one day came a messenger from England from King Henry II, begging that one of the monks ordained in that order be sent to England to found a monastery. Hugh was chosen, and with great regret he left his beloved refuge and went forth to serve others. He built the monastery, and strove to give his monks a real love of the rule which was a rigid one. Later he was called to be Bishop of Lincoln, and with his own hands he helped to build its great cathedral.

"And what of the swan, Brother Stephen?" asked Johanna.

"A great wild white swan that lived in a lake near the bishop's palace would allow only St. Hugh to touch him. When St. Hugh was at home, the swan would be near by, but when he was away, it would escape to its wild haunts, always to reappear when St. Hugh was expected to return and be the first to greet him."

"And dost thou really think St. Hugh always regretted having left Grande Chartreuse and having come to England?"

"Nay," answered Brother Stephen quickly, "he was ready to serve God here, and he loved his people, but his spirit longed for the deep meditation of that great, silent monastery. When the day came for him to go to be consecrated into the new office of Bishop of Lincoln, horsemen arrived to conduct him in state to London. They were mounted on magnificent horses, richly caparisoned, and in their midst on muleback rode good St. Hugh, bareheaded and simply clad, with a bundle of sheepskins which was his bed, fastened on behind."

"Is it not true, Brother Stephen, that some men are born to be saints, whereas others may be born to be – Merchant Adventurers, mayhap?" and Johanna watched Brother Stephen's face closely as she said this.

"There is more than one way of serving God in this world, Johanna, but I can lead thee to Him only by ways of the spirit. Thou must learn of the good ways of the world from another teacher than I."

"But thou hast seen the world, Brother Stephen. Thou hast wandered far."

"Ay," answered Brother Stephen. "I have sailed over many leagues of water and have trod many stretches of desolate land to pray and fast in the holy places." With his back to the sun he lifted his head, and looked off. "Far, far to the east is the Holy Land, and the hearts of men are still ringing with the cry of the First Crusade! It is the Will of God!"

"But what is to the west?" Johanna asked suddenly with childlike impetuosity, and turned to look full into the glory of the setting sun.

Just then the convent bell rang for vespers, and Brother Stephen, slowly shaking his head, picked up his spade and withdrew, repeating over and over again, "It is the Will of God! It is the Will of God!"

So indeed did the saints look to the East and the Holy Land, but the Merchant Adventurers came to look to the great unknown West which had yet to be explored and settled, and on the lips of many of them were the words of the First Crusade, "God Wills It."

CHAPTER VIII. LORD ARUNDEL IN THE FENS

LORD ARUNDEL left by Wormgate, as he was instructed, shortly before noon. He was rather filled with misgivings, for he knew enough of Prince Henry's ways to feel that they might lead the man who took them into unfamiliar and somewhat hazardous places, but underneath his fine clothes Lord Arundel carried a stout heart and one that was not averse to a moderate degree of adventure.

"'Twill be worth something if indeed the payment will cover a new outfit of clothes," he thought, as he pushed the skiff out into the river and took up the oars. "To do that it must be around two marks, and I was but thinking yesterday that I should have a hard time securing that amount for several months yet."

Below at the quay many ships and fishing boats were at anchor, and traders and shipmen were actively plying back and forth in small boats laden with bales and barrels. Soon Lord Arundel passed beyond all this, and as the current was strong, he tucked up his sleeves and set himself to work at the oars.

"He said to take the inlet by the large oak tree, and there it is ahead," he muttered between pulls. "Then must I paddle and pole through a shallow lagoon, and so through the reeds and rushes into a small lake." He rested a moment on his oars and shook out his tunic that it might not get into great disorder. "What strikes me as a little uncommon is that a fenman, and an honest one at that, should have as much as two marks to lay in a wager. If he were not honest, it would not be so hard to believe, but being honest, as the prince claims him to be, it is a large amount to expect him to hand over, and if he were dishonest, he would not be likely to pay it. However, I can but do as the prince said and wait to see the results."

Now Lord Arundel ceased to wonder at other than the pleasant country around him. His way took him between dark green alders and pale green reeds, where the coot clanked, and the bittern boomed, and the sedge bird, not content with its own sweet song, mocked the song of the other birds around. From afar came the wild whistle of the curlew and the trumpet note of the great white swan. It was a sunny expanse of fertile marshland adorned with goodly trees.

In the willow grove Tod of the Fens and Tom True Tongue were concerned over the recovering of an eel trap, a device made of reeds and twigs which was baited with small fish and sunk several feet below the surface among the reeds.

"It is a large and lively one which we have caught this day," said Tod as he pulled up the trap with great difficulty.

"Ho there!" called a voice which startled Tod so that he reversed the trap, and the eel fell at his feet. Without a moment's delay he stepped hard upon it as did likewise Tom True Tongue on another part of the slippery creature, and then they both looked up. Lord Arundel swung around in the skiff and faced them.

"Art thou Tod of the Fens?" he asked, "thou with the shaggy locks?"

"Ay," answered Tod in surprise, "that is my name."

"Thy locks would be quite in style, forsooth, if thou didst but brush them and curl them a bit," and Lord Arundel surveyed him critically. "'Twould not be so bad!" Then he turned to Tom True Tongue. "And thou – why, it seems as if I had seen thee before. Canst thou be Tom True Tongue or Tongue Tie?"

"Ay."

"And where have I seen thee? Egad! I know now! Thou art the rogue who set us astray in the fens."

"And who is it that has set thee astray here?" asked Tom.

"A man thou dost call Dismas. But help me ashore, and I promise not to beat thee as I said I would should I see thee again."

Tod and Tom looked at each other, then at the still squirming eel, and then at Lord Arundel.

"Thou canst beach thyself yonder," said Tod. "We can do nothing for thee until we have finished with this eel and skinned him."

"I am like to get my shoes in the mud if I do try to land myself," complained Lord Arundel.

"Well, then, thou canst sit out there until we have finished."

"The sun will fade the scarlet of my houppelande, and sunburn my nose to an unbecoming degree. I will come in myself since I must."

Tod smiled broadly.

"Dismas has not done so badly," he whispered. "I can see sport ahead."

"I, too," answered Tom.

In another moment Lord Arundel's voice was heard a short distance away. "Help!" he called in tones of distress. "'Tis just as I said. I have one foot ashore, and it has sunk in to the ankle. Here am I astride the skiff, and I can neither go nor come."

"Thou canst not have chosen a good place," called back Tod, peering through the leaves, and then he burst into a loud laugh at the sight he saw. One of Lord Arundel's feet was indeed well sunk in the mud, and balancing himself with one hand on the bow, the other foot in the skiff, he was trying to keep his long houppelande from trailing in the water.

"Thou didst not come in a good boating costume," called Tod. "Thy red leg is the wise one, for it would not venture forth, but thy blue leg is indeed in trouble. Go help him, Tom."

"Ay, and be quick about it," called Lord Arundel desperately, "for the skiff is moving out and my legs are at odds in more than color."

Tom True Tongue, convulsed with laughter, hurried to his rescue, and with a stout stick he was able to assist the scarlet leg of Lord Arundel's parti-colored hose to a hard bit of ground, and then pulling together they freed the blue leg. Lord Arundel sank down on the ground, his blue leg with its besmeared shoe, dangling gold chain, and water-soaked point stretched out beside the still immaculate scarlet leg.

"Didst ever see such destruction?" he lamented. "How can I ever appear at Bolingbroke in such a state?"

Tom pulled up the skiff, and Tod came around, holding the eel, now entirely prepared for cooking, on the end of a stick.

"And why has Dismas sent thee here?" asked Tod.

"These be the words he told me to say," answered Lord Arundel, "'Dismas was delayed and could not keep the tryst. I am come at his bidding to take the payment Tom True Tongue would give, for which thou must notch his tally once more.' Those be his words, but I must add that I hope the payment will cover a new blue leg to these hose as well as a new attire. How much is it?"

"How much is what?" asked Tom in amazement, "I do not understand."

"I might say thou art famous for that, for thou didst not understand the last time I had discourse with thee. Mayhap thou art dreaming again."

"Ay, perhaps I be," answered Tom, rubbing his hand over his close-cropped hair which was trimmed high above his ears in quite the opposite extreme to Tod's. "What sayest thou, Tod?"

"I think I see," answered Tod slowly. "See if this be right. Dismas could not come himself and so he sent thee to pay the wager which he lost to Tom True Tongue here."

"Lost? For shame! dost think to fool me? 'Twas won, and the amount was to be paid me. Come, now, do not think to cheat me out of anything, for he promised on his honor that thou wert fair and honest."

"What was the payment that he named?"

"He named no exact amount except that it would vouchsafe me a new attire."

At these words Tod let out a roar and so did Tom True Tongue, for now they knew what Dismas had meant. Lord Arundel looked on in amazement. Then as the shouts continued, he began to get angry.

"Egad! what fools ye be to rant around and toss your heads like baited bulls. I see naught to laugh at. Besides, the fog is rolling in, and I would have the money and be off to Horncastle, where I am told ye will guide me."

The fog was indeed rolling in, for the sun was fast disappearing and the willow grove itself was fading away into soft grayness.

"Thou canst not make Horncastle this afternoon, even with us to guide thee," Tod told him. "'Twould be useless to try. Do thou stay here until the fog lifts, and in the meantime we shall see about this payment."

"Ah, well!" sighed Lord Arundel, "if I must, I must; but I do hope thou art prepared to feed me, for I am quite empty."

"We are well supplied with fish and eel and waterfowl so that thou needst not starve."

Lord Arundel was about to speak again, when suddenly he turned and through the fog behind him enormous figures loomed up, indistinguishable except in their great height and breadth.

"How now!" ejaculated Lord Arundel, "is this place inhabited by giants? We are being beset by some strange creatures," and he jumped to his feet and set his back to a near-by tree trunk. On came the dark masses, and the foremost one broke through the mist. It was Heron mounted on stilts and carrying his skiff on his back, held there by a strong thong bound to his forehead. Behind him were several other members of the band, likewise burdened and mounted. They dropped their skiffs and dismounted, whereupon Lord Arundel again found his voice.

"Dost mean to say thou canst walk about the fens like that?"

Heron turned at his words, for he had not seen that there was a stranger present. He eyed him in surprise.

"It is no more strange than that thou canst walk about the fens in those things," he commented, when his eye fell on the elegant shoes with their enormously long toes.

"A match! a match!" called Tom True Tongue suddenly. "Heron and this stranger to run a race! The stranger on stilts, and Heron in his outfit. The prize, the longest pike which has been caught this day!"

The band of fenmen cheered and all looked to Lord Arundel to see what he would say. His face was full of seriousness, while Heron's was wreathed in a broad grin.

"Come now, 'tis not such a bad idea, after all," said Lord Arundel, "but there is nothing to prevent his winning that I can see. He has the advantage. Moreover, 'twill not be so very good for my fine clothes, for belike he will stretch and split them all to pieces."

"If thou wilt agree to this entertainment," said Tod, "we will dismiss the payment that Dismas intended for thee, and thou mayhap wilt be better off."

"And how is that?" asked Lord Arundel, raising his eyebrows and turning upon Tod with an air of disbelief.

"Because Dismas and Tom True Tongue held a wager that the one could fool more people in a week and a day than the other. The time was up night before last so that Tom True Tongue wins, for Dismas did not come. The loser was to be ducked in our ducking stool which we have yonder in the bog-hole. Which dost thou prefer for thy fine clothes, the ducking stool or the race?"

It did not take Lord Arundel long to decide.

"Marry! the race, by all means. I did not think it of him, but now 'tis as clear as yon muddy bog-hole, but what causes the mud is the thought that I could be so outdone!"

With many sighs and groans Lord Arundel set to work to remove his clothes, and as he took off each piece, he held it up for careful inspection, as a clothier would his wares, that no fine detail might be overlooked.

"Dost see this pattern in gold thread?" he asked as he removed his houppelande, and revealed the under tunic with its long tight sleeves, "and this gold button at the wrist? Take care now thou dost not burst that off."

At last, after more cautioning and delay, Heron stood dressed in Lord Arundel's clothes and Lord Arundel in Heron's coarse tunic, while the band looked on in great merriment. Heron scarcely dared to breathe, for the costume strained at every point, and his long toes from which the chains had been removed to make the race more even, tripped him up when he moved.

"Come now, Sir Popinjay, art thou so lost in those clothes that thou canst not find thyself?" shouted Wat, dancing around him and slapping his sides with mirth.

"Nay," answered Lord Arundel dismally, "but I might wish I were. Fetch me those stilts and help me to mount."

"Not here," said Heron, "let us to yonder straight stretch where the ground is not soft."

"And the race shall be to the oak tree and back," announced Tom True Tongue, "for beyond that we could not see well and the sight would be wasted."

With the help of Wat and Bat at the sides, Lord Arundel mounted the stilts, but before the word could be said to start, he had come down again, stepping so hard on Bat's toe that Bat caught it up in his hand and hopped around, his mouth drawn up into a grimace of pain. The same thing happened again, but this time Wat was the sufferer.

"Here, Sir Popinjay, I will not help thee more," said Wat, limping off in disgust. "Do thou mount thyself!"

"Ah, well, what must be, must," sighed Lord Arundel, and he rose again on the stilts.

"Go!" shrieked Tod in haste while he saw him still in the air. Off went Heron, the long houppelande caught up over his arm, the turban-like hat slipping over his forehead, and the liripipe floating out behind. Lord Arundel still stood balancing, until Heron had gone several rods, had stepped on the end of his right toe with his left foot and fallen with a thud and the loud sound of ripping. The fenmen rolled around with laughter, which was silenced suddenly and amazingly. Lord Arundel started off, and with swift strides he stepped over the prostrate Heron, gained the oak, and returned before Heron had time to rise, or the echo of the fenmen's laughter to have more than just died away.

Lord Arundel dismounted and hurried to Heron.

"Now out of those clothes before thou dost them any more harm," he commanded. "I have beat thee."

The band cheered lustily and gathered around.

"Ay, thou art indeed beaten, and thou wilt do well if thou canst beat him on stilts," cried Tod. "Never have I seen greater skill. Long live Sir Popinjay!"

"And long live Dismas!" said Tom True Tongue, "for he, too, could vie with us in our sport."

Lord Arundel was in the best of spirits.

"The pike is mine and I would eat it now."

"Thou shalt," said Tod, "and thou shalt have back thine own clothes without more delay. I will not deny thou didst fool me, and the man who fools Tod of the Fens can be master of the band."

"Nay, 'tis not the life for me," said Lord Arundel, "but thou canst entertain me this evening, and set me on my way to-morrow."

Wat and Bat were the only ones who were not entirely delighted with Sir Popinjay.

"He did not need to step so on our toes," they grumbled.

Lord Arundel heard them.

"Perhaps I did not need to," he agreed, "but then I've no doubt it has made ye both better mannered, and there was need enough of that."

The rest of the afternoon and evening was spent eating and drinking and making merry. Lord Arundel told tales of castle and court life, and the fenmen told of their life in the open, of the water-fowl and their habits, of the tides of the Lindis, especially the "bird tide," so called because it came at midsummer when the birds were hatching their eggs, and was so low that the marshes were free from tidal waters, and the birds were undisturbed.

Throughout it all, Lord Arundel did not once reveal who he or Dismas was; nor did the fenmen ask, for the concealing of identity was a recognized privilege, and men could come among them without fear of being tracked beyond their going.

Tom True Tongue showed the badge which Dismas had given him.

"Dismas said that if I wished to find him out, this badge would help me, but that will I not do. Though he did not keep the tryst, he has given us a merrier time than we have had for many a month, and I no longer bear him any grudge." So saying he skimmed the badge into the darkness, and as the clear "plop" which it made as it struck the water came back to their ears, Lord Arundel jokingly said, "Though thou art now Tom-who-does-not-lie, some day mayhap thou wilt be as I have said, Tom Tongue Tie!"

CHAPTER IX. THE EASTERLINGS IN ANOTHER ROLE

LORD ARUNDEL was well escorted by the fen-men to Horncastle early the next morning, but Tod himself did not go with them. Instead he betook himself by skiff across the lake and out into the river.

"I would I had thought to follow Dismas more closely," he was thinking, as he poled his skiff among tall reeds, "but I doubt if it takes me long to discover what he has been about. I'll interview Simon Gough, for there is not much that escapes him."

Simon Gough was in a good frame of mind this morning, and ready for a chat with Tod of the Fens. "How now," he greeted him, "'tis some time since thou hast gladdened me with the sight of that rough head of thine. What hast thou been about, thou and that waggish band of thine? Marry, if thou hadst been in this town this fortnight past, thou wouldst have had enough to suit even thy highly flavored taste for oddity."

"How so?" Tod inquired eagerly, as he sat himself down on the stone step of the gatehouse.

"Hast thou not heard the town coffer has been robbed?"

"It cannot be!" expostulated Tod.

"Ay," answered Simon, "four of the town officers and the bailiff himself were robbed of their keys in full daylight in the streets of the town, and no violence done. They say it was the work of five men, a chapman, a peasant, a friar, an apprentice lad, and a minstrel but – " Here Simon Gough looked around to see that no one was within hearing. "Canst keep a secret?" he asked in a whisper. "I have told no man, but would tell thee, for thou hast a head for such things, and I would like to know what thou dost make of it."

"Thou knowest me well enough to know that I am not the man to spread news. Out with thy secret if thou wilt!"

"By my troth, it was all done by one man in all those disguises who came in over this bridge of mine!" and Simon leaned over and whispered in Tod's ear this bit of information.

"Well, how now!"

"'Tis the truth I speak, and to prove it the rascal did fear that I did know him, and so what does he do but seal my lips with two good nobles — "

"Which I warrant did not seal them but opened them to many a tankard of good ale," interposed Tod with a smile.

Simon smacked his lips. "But what dost thou make of it?" he pursued. "He was a lean young man with blue eyes and high cheek-bones."

Simon, now that he had begun, was loath to stop, and Tod heard from beginning to end the whole story. Tod was thinking hard.

"And so the town coffer lies empty?" Tod spoke slowly and watched Simon's face as he spoke.

"So they say," answered Simon, "two hundred marks gone and they think it was the work of five men, but I tell thee, 'tis not so! 'Twas one only, and a clever fellow he is, too!"

"Ay," acquiesced Tod, "if what thou sayest is true he is a bold thief and will probably live to be a penitent one."

He rose to leave, for he had heard everything Simon had to tell him and he had much to think about. Surely the Prince of Wales would not rob the town coffer. He had known the madcap prince the moment he had seen him, and had not his riddle shown the prince that he knew him? What was it that walked before Dismas and would walk before even the prince himself? The answer was Dismas's shadow, for his and the prince's were one and the same, and the prince had understood.

"But thou hast not said what thou dost make of it?" Simon queried.

"I know not what to make of it," Tod answered slowly. "If the town coffer lies empty where lies the blame?"

Simon shook his head.

"Sir Frederick Tilney is likely to be the one to bear the brunt of this," Tod commented.

"How so?"

"Hast thou yet to learn that when blame is floating around loose, 'tis usually on the shoulders of the most prosperous that it finally lodges itself?"

"Belike, belike," Simon agreed. "But if he does become involved in this, and anything I can tell will be of help to him, then shall I speak."

Tod thought for a moment. "If thou wilt take my advice, thou wilt say nothing to any one no matter what happens," he said slowly. "'Twill but put thyself in a bad light forsooth, for it will show that thou dost love thine ale more than the discharge of thy duty of guarding the town."

Simon became uneasy. "I had not thought of that. Thou wilt not tell what I have told thee?"

"Nay," answered Tod. "I promise thee I will keep thy secret. Have no fear."

So Tod left, assured that Simon would do nothing that might lead men to seek a tall, lean young man with eyes deep-set under shaggy eyebrows whom some indeed might recognize even as he had. Tod whistled softly to himself. "This indeed is royal foolery," he thought, "and it would seem as if he were in truth the Prince of Madcaps!"

He wandered into the market place and thought that he would stop at the "Golden Fleece" for a draught of ale. As he drew near, he saw a group of Easterlings, drinking at the large outside table, their pointed and beribboned sugar-loaf hats assuring him even from a distance that they were foreigners. Tod's eye was caught and held by the one who sat at the farther end of the table. He was large and heavily built with a round face and thick jaw. Having seen him, Tod decided not to stop at the tavern, but continued on through the square and out toward St. John's gate.

"Mayhap I have seen him before!" he muttered to himself, "and the sight of him again makes the world seem less fair!"

To the shipyard went Tod. A ship was being built there, none other indeed than Sir Frederick's, and Tod immediately fell into conversation with the workmen, and many were the questions he asked.

“One can see that thou dost know something of ships and the sea,” one of them said, as he turned on the ladder on which he stood, and looked Tod over from the top of his shining head to the end of his muddy leggings. “Sir Frederick is on the lookout for a good shipmaster.”

Although the idea was a new one to Tod, it took root fast, and on the way back through the warehouses, he sought out Sir Frederick. What went on

AN EASTERLING.

between them must have been to their mutual liking, for although Sir Frederick’s face was serious when Tod left him, his words showed confidence.

“And I can trust thee to return as soon as thou hast word to bring.”

That evening Tod took his band by surprise.

“Look ye here!” he exclaimed suddenly, “’tis an idle life we lead. Come now, we need not reveal what we would not, but how many of ye have had a taste of seafaring? Hands up!"

Hands went up. Of the band, twelve strong, all but two responded.

"'Twas a good life, after all," said Tom True Tongue, "for indeed it does take men to play it, and none of thy castle-bred retainers."

"Still harboring thoughts against Dismas and Sir Popinjay!" laughed Heron.

"I am aggrieved that they should have come upon us, and played our game, and then gone thence. Does make our game seem poor enough, methinks," growled Tom True Tongue.

Tod's mind was on other things. "How many of ye have drunk from Stortebecker's goblet?"

"The 'Victual Brothers!'" shouted Heron. "Come, now, if thou knowest aught of them, out with it!"

"Hast played with them or against them?" asked another.

The "Victual Brothers" was the name of a famous band of pirates which a few years before this time had invested the Baltic Sea. Their rise to power had come about in this way: King Waldemar, the young and daring King of Denmark, had defied the great Hanseatic League by sacking the town of Wisby on the island of Gothland, which was the richest town belonging to the League. King Waldemar had gathered a great army and told them he would lead them to a place where there was so much gold and silver that even the pigs ate out of silver troughs. The year before crafty King Waldemar had disguised himself as a merchant and visited Wisby. Having secured the love of a goldsmith's daughter, he learned from her the secret of the defenses of the island and the town. Confident then of success, he took his army to Gothland. A bloody battle took place outside the walls of Wisby, and to-day a cross marks the place where eighteen thousand Gothlanders fell in defense of their town. Waldemar was victorious, and commanding a breach to be made in the wall for his triumphal entry, he encouraged his greedy army to plunder and sack unmercifully. Sailing away with his ships heavily laden with gold and silver, and with two mighty carbuncles taken from the windows of St. Nicholas' Church, Waldemar was destined to regret his misdeeds. A mighty storm arose, and the Danish ships with their plunder were lost. It is said that the great carbuncles which formerly served to light seamen into the harbor of Wisby, now on still clear nights gleam from the bottom of the ocean.

This act of Waldemar's brought about a great war between Denmark and the Hanseatic League. To aid them in this war, the Hansa had openly countenanced piracy as long as it was directed against Danish ships, and a large number of adventurers had banded together. Commissioned by the League to supply provisions to a certain part of the Swedish coast, they had become known as the "Victual Brothers," but their real business was piracy. They took Gothland for their stronghold and became masters of the Baltic Sea.

The leader of this band was Godeke Michelson, and he was joined by a young German noble who had wasted away his wealth, and wished to take part in the wild, adventuresome life. This noble was so strong that he could break iron chains asunder, and he drank so deeply that the goblet from which he drank was known for its great size, and few other men could hope to empty it. Thus came the name he took, Stortebecker, which means "drink bumpers down," and often the captives he took could save their lives only if they could empty Stortebecker's goblet.

When the war with Denmark came to a successful end, it was difficult for the League to wipe out the piracy which they had allowed to flourish. Godeke and Stortebecker had to be captured and executed.

In reply to the fenman's question, "Didst thou play with them or against them?" Tod held up his right hand, which bore the deep scar in the palm. "This may bear witness that my past is not without its stain, but at least ye may all be sure I was no pirate. I will tell ye this much: I was there when Stortebecker was brought in chains to the headsman, and one of his followers saw I this day in Boston, one whom I have cause to remember well. Now he goes by the name of Ranolf and is master of one of the ships of the Hansa."

"Sayest thou so?" exclaimed Tom True Tongue. "Do they think to make a pirate into an honest shipmaster?"

"I know not what they think," answered Tod, "but this do I think. Given a good English ship, I know of nothing I had rather do than take to the sea again. 'Tis a hard life and a dangerous one, but when the call comes, it is a strong one and cannot be resisted."

"Couldst thou take the office of master?"

"Ay, that I could, and have in the past," answered Tod. "Which of all of ye have ever been steersman?"

"I," spoke up Tom True Tongue and Heron together.

"Good," burst out Tod heartily. "'Tis better than I even dared hope. How many of ye would ship with me, given the opportunity?"

Up went every hand, and the men fell into excited talking and questioning.

"Dost think thou canst get a ship?" asked Wat.

"Ay, and a Boston one it will be!"

"The one that is now building?"

Tod nodded in assent.

"'Twas a lucky day that did jar our content," sighed Tom True Tongue. "Here have we lived this long time like frogs sunning on a lily pad, and we might never have realized the sun had gone in and it was time to jump in again, had not — "

"Had not Dismas and Sir Popinjay come our way," added Heron.

"Why wilt thou not tell us something of thy life at sea?" asked Bat of Tod.

Tod tossed his head and wrinkled up his smooth forehead. His eyes wandered off across the fens to where St. Botolph's lantern sent its steady light off across the Wash.

"Many's the time I have been glad enough to see that light," he remarked thoughtfully. "I am not a man of many words, but if ye would hear, I'll tell ye this."

The men drew around and, throwing more sticks on the fire, they sat down to listen to this adventure.

A small English ship under the mastership of Nicholas Beckman set out from Cornwall for Bergen with a cargo of tin. It was early in the season, and the North Sea was full of floating ice. The crew consisted of eight men, among them one whose name was Todhunter, who was none other than our Tod of the Fens. English seamen knew well that the Victual Brothers were their foes, for one of their interests was to harry them and discourage any attempt they might make to vie with the Hanseatic League in its trade with Norway. When they were still several leagues from Bergen, a ship was seen bearing down on them. It was a queer, awkward craft, but amazingly well-handled in the rough sea. One sail it had, and rowers' benches.

"What chance have we in an encounter with yonder pirate ship?" Todhunter asked Beckman, whose eyes had first sighted the sail, and never for a moment left it.

"'Twill be well to give over!" he answered shortly.

"Thou wouldst not put up a fight?" asked Todhunter in amazement, and then he broke out wrathfully. "Wouldst give over without a fight to those villainous pirates, and we a stout body of Englishmen?"

"Who is the master of this ship?" demanded Beckman. "Do as I say. Give over at the first demand. Show no fight."

The pirate ship crossed the bow, and for a moment was lost in a deep trough in the sea, only the top of its mast giving evidence of its whereabouts. The next instant the sea rolled away before it. The grappling iron shot out and fell athwart the English ship. Side by side the two ships tossed. Amid the flapping of the rigging and the roar of the sea, human voices bellowed.

"What cargo?"

"The best of English tin."

"We shall unload her."

"Ay."

"Dost mean ye will give over?"

"Ay," bellowed Beckman, "wouldst unload now in this sea?"

"Nay, we will put in!"

With these words the pirate ship set about towing the smaller craft. The sea was heavy, and the men strained at the great oars. Soon they worked in to the lee side of a rugged promontory.

"Surely we do outnumber them," urged Todhunter. "Why can we not set upon them when they board us?" Beckman gave no sign of consent. "I do truly believe thou art in league with them," Todhunter muttered under his breath, but Beckman did not hear. The other members of the crew were likewise sullen and disturbed.

The pirate ship dropped anchor, and Beckman did likewise. Then swarming over the sides, the pirates fell upon the Englishmen. Their weapons were taken, and they were bound hand and foot.

Then it was easy to see that there was treachery. There was consultation between Beckman and Ranolf, for he it was who was in command of the pirate ship.

Todhunter lay on his side and watched the bars of metal being loaded on to the pirate ship. Near him young Desmond, who had been steersman, lay wrenching at the cords that bound him and cursing loudly.

After the cargo had been removed, the pirates hoisted anchor, and off they sailed, taking Beckman with them. "Good luck to ye all!" he shouted, "and may ye return whence ye came, and bring as fine a cargo with ye again that we may relieve ye of it!"

"A set of fools we be!" Todhunter groaned. "Here shall we lie and die before we can get ourselves free."

"Let's be thankful we were not pitched overboard with no chance of our lives!" called another of the crew.

"We might as well have been," groaned another. "Then it would have been over soon."

It was then noon, for it had been early morning when the pirate ship had sighted them and towed them in to this sheltered bay. Sea birds had gathered and were screaming and circling overhead. The sky was a deep blue, and against it the black, ragged cliffs stood out in relentless rigidity. On the windward side of the promontory the surf boiled and churned with an angry roar and crash.

"Can none of ye break loose?" shouted Todhunter.

"Nay," came the groaning reply from the men. "The chains do bite our wrists until the blood runs freely."

"Is there no man whose hands are bound with rope?"

"Ay," answered Desmond, lying nearest to Todhunter. "Mine are, but I cannot burst them."

Todhunter lay and thought a while. Now the birds came flapping around the ship, a host of them, and some lighted on the men. They rolled over to protect their faces, and their groanings became louder.

"This is what those fiends have left us to," roared Todhunter, raising himself and lunging desperately at three birds which were hanging over him. "They will peck the flesh off our bones while yet we live! Have ye a tinder box?" he asked suddenly.

"Ay," answered Desmond.

"If we could kindle a blaze, maphap thou couldst burn thy ropes off. 'Tis our only hope, I do believe!"

He rolled across the intervening space and fell across Desmond. The birds flapped and shrieked. More and more of them had gathered so that their wings cut off the sun, and they seemed to hang like a menacing cloud over the ship. The men fought them off desperately but unavailingly. They rolled about in the vain hope of finding protection. The pirates had left the hatchway blocked. One man, exhausted and terrified, and already frightfully wounded by the birds, with a curse and a prayer flung himself over the ship's side. Another was about to follow his example, but Todhunter called to him.

"Bear up but a little longer, and we may all be saved. I have the tinder box."

"Wouldst set me ablaze?" Desmond asked in amazement.

"Thou couldst not be worse off than thou art now, forsooth, even though thou didst burn," Tod answered relentlessly. "If we can char thy ropes a bit, thou couldst break them asunder."

After many unsuccessful attempts Tod finally succeeded in striking sparks with the flint and steel. The tinder caught, and fanned by the wings of the hovering birds, it blazed up, and caught Tod's rough jacket. Desmond managed to get his hands into the burning cloth.

"Heaven help us!" he muttered. "It will burn my wrist through before it finds the ropes."

"To say nothing of my back," groaned Todhunter.

The smoke kept the birds away from them. The fire was creeping up Tod's arms. His back was well ablaze. Desmond gave a great groan and wrenched at the ropes. They gave, and, with a shout, he set about smothering the flames. In another moment Desmond had his feet free and was working at Tod's chains. Both men forgot their aching hands and blistered backs, as they hastened to help the others. They fought away the birds with oars and chains. A wild cheer went up as all the men stood free.

The birds understood that they had lost their prey. They screamed about the rigging with hoarse, mournful cries, then rose in a flock and departed like a gray cloud over the promontory. Many of them lay dead on the deck or struggled wounded in the water.

There was no food or water on board, as the pirates had taken everything. The men were faint and weak. Two days later they reached Bergen, as gaunt and weary a crew as ever made port. Another English ship gave them aid, and under Todhunter's command, they returned to England.

"I should think the shrieking of these birds would set thy skin to twitching," said Tom True Tongue, when Tod had finished.

"Not so much as the sight of Ranolf, forsooth," answered Tod, "and I doubt not if Beckman himself was far away."

"But how camest thou to see Stortebecker?" asked Wat. "Was he as powerful a giant as he was said to be?"

"Ay, for hast thou not heard that he and Michelson bore the bones of St. Vincent against their breasts, the bones which they stole from a shrine in Spain? Those bones endowed them with superhuman strength."

"Then how came they ever to have been captured?"

"A Hamburg alderman set forth in the 'Colored Cow,' and came upon Stortebecker's ship one night at dusk off the coast of Norway. A courageous sailor poured molten lead upon the rudder, so that the ship became unseaworthy, and after a three days' battle, Stortebecker and his crew were captured, and taken upon the 'Colored Cow' back to Hamburg. No treasure was found upon his ship, but when he was taken up for trial, he promised for his freedom a chain of gold and silver long enough to span the whole town of Hamburg. This did not tempt his judges, so he and his companions, dressed in their finest and gayest of clothes, were led to the executioner. It was later discovered that the mast of his ship was filled with molten gold, and there was indeed enough to make a chain which would span the town of Hamburg."

The tongues of the fenmen were loosened, and story followed upon story. Unnoticed by the others, Tod had drawn Tom True Tongue aside.

"To-morrow," Tod said to him, "we must set out for Castle Bolingbroke."

"Why so?" asked Tom True Tongue in surprise.

"It is necessary that I find Dismas, and I would take thee for company."

"Would that I had kept that badge he gave me, for 'twould have made our search the easier."

"Never fear," answered Tod, "for well I know that if we once gain Bolingbroke, 'twill not be hard to find Dismas's whereabouts."

CHAPTER X. AT CASTLE BOLINGBROKE

TOD and Tom True Tongue set off early the next morning with stilts and skiff. By means of these they were able to short-cut the distance between Boston and Castle Bolingbroke. It was before noon when they finally left the stilts and skiff in concealment, and passing through the small village which had grown up around the castle, took to the main highway that approached it from the southwest.

Castle Bolingbroke with its towers and rampart walls was situated in a hollow surrounded by hills on all sides but the one that opened to the vast, inaccessible stretch of fens and the distant town of Boston. Even on this sunny morning all was grim and cold about it, except for the silver flash of the pigeons circling about the gaunt, triangular tower at the southeast corner.

"Alackaday!" groaned Tod, "I have not much liking for this day's business. The very sight of yonder fortress clouds the sun and sets my heart to thumping."

"'Tis not too late to turn back," answered Tom True Tongue. "I know naught of castle life, and it does not suit me to be gaped at by royal flunkies, and how dost think we shall ever find Dismas or Sir Popinjay?"

"Tush!" answered Tod. "Trust me to find them and to outgape the best of them. Stiffen thyself and come along!"

Even as they approached the drawbridge a company of horsemen came riding out. There was much gayety, for the day was fine, and they were off with falcons tied to their wrists. Foremost on a fine white horse rode none other than Lord Arundel, smartly clad in a hunting suit of Lincoln green.

"Fortune favors us!" Tod exclaimed. "Here comes the gay-feathered bird himself."

As Lord Arundel approached, Tod stepped up to his horse's head. Lord Arundel drew up. He looked at Tod, and then at Tom True Tongue.

"What!" he exclaimed as he recognized them both. "Am I dreaming?"

The other horsemen circled around.

"Nay," answered Tod quickly and in a low voice, "we have come hither seeking Dismas, for I have need of a word with him. Wilt thou lead us to him?"

"That I cannot," answered Lord Arundel quickly, "for he is off making war in Wales. Off with the Prince of Wales he is!"

Tod's face fell. "Well, then, my business will have to wait, and we will betake ourselves back the way we have come."

"Nay," answered Lord Arundel quickly. "Now thou art here, think not I shall let thee go so easily. Thou didst entertain me in the fens, and now shall we entertain thee, thee and thy dreaming friend!" He turned to his surprised followers. "Would ye give up your hawking for sport of another kind?" he asked. "I promise ye it will be worth it. Do ye remember this wag?" and his gesture picked out Tom True Tongue, who stood at a distance.

"He is the man who sent us splashing through the fens but a few days past," some one answered.

"Ay," assented others of the party.

"He has not so merry a look to-day methinks!" another said, as he circled around on his restive horse.

"If thou shouldst ask me, I would say he does look more wide-awake when he is dreaming."

"Come, let us wake him up!" several shouted together, and wheeling their horses about, they cut off the retreat of the protesting fenmen and carried them before them over the drawbridge.

Once inside the castle yard, the surprised stableboys took the horses and falcons, and surrounded by the young noblemen, Tod and Tom True Tongue had the appearance of culprits brought to justice.

"How now!" grumbled Tom when he had a chance to get a word into Tod's ear, "what are we in for now?"

"Do thy best whate'er it be!" Tod muttered back.

"Now," said Lord Arundel in the best of humor, "the stilt race that I have told ye of was this man's idea," and he dug Tom True Tongue with his elbow. "He was awake then and did run around and slap his sides with mirth."

"Mayhap a whack of the sandbag of the quintain would be good for him," some gay voice suggested.

"Let us see if he can read the motto on the fountain in the garden," put in another.

"Not so bad for a beginning," agreed Lord Arundel, "but," he added with a wink of the eye farther from Tom True Tongue, "of course there be naught to that but child's play. Any fool can step up and look at words that be written plain."

Forthwith he led the way through the king's own quarters, then unoccupied and meager in their furnishings, to the privy garden which was separated by a wall from the open space of the castle grounds.

The garden was bright with spring flowers, and bees hummed in the blossoming fruit trees. Vines clambered over the walls, and the warm sun settled down here as if it was the one place in the whole grim castle where it could enter in and receive no rebuff.

"Seest thou the fountain?" Lord Arundel said, taking the reluctant Tom True Tongue by the arm and walking with him toward a structure of stone which stood against the wall at one end. The figure on it was of a laughing faun. "The motto is about laughter, and seeing that thou knowest something about it indeed, do thou step up and read it to us."

"Nay," expostulated Tom True Tongue, "I have but little skill at reading," and he held back.

"Thou canst spell it out, forsooth," urged another.

With hesitation Tom True Tongue stepped nearer, while the others drew back somewhat. Just as Tom's eye reached the right level, and he took a step nearer to see what he could make of the letters, out from the mouth of the grinning face, which up to this time had been spouting harmlessly, came a torrent of water which struck Tom full and fair on his close-cropped head.

"Ha! ha! ha!" shouted the onlookers who had retired to even a safer distance, and Tod outroared the best of them, as Tom, with water dripping from his very finger tips, turned, and stepping again on the fatal tile under which was concealed the device which caused this to happen, received another great deluge on the back of his head. Stamping and shaking himself, he drove the others ahead of him as he walked away from the fountain.

"That is the pet delight of Prince Hal," announced one of the youths. "Would that he had been here, for never have I seen it work so well! Ho! ho!"

Tom True Tongue was not angry but greatly amused at his own misfortune. "Did I not say I had no fondness for learning? This is but another attempt that has dampened me down."

"Now thou hast one eye open at least, hast thou not? We'll pry up the other in the tilting yard mayhap, and then we'll feed thee well, and so to sleep again if thou wouldst."

As they crossed the paved castle yard, still talking and laughing, Lord Arundel who was in the front of the party was suddenly tripped up, and sent sprawling. "The hare, the hare!" he cried, and all the young stopped short, for out from under their very feet sprang a large hare, speeding for the steps leading down to the prison room.

"He went in there," shouted one of the youths, pointing to the room at the head of the steps. "I saw him go in."

"Let's after him, for there is no outlet," cried another.

Picking himself up, Lord Arundel led the chase. "Do ye all stand on guard and let him not escape, while I fetch some of the hounds," one man suggested, and hurried off to the stables.

He was soon back with two hounds straining at the leash that held them.

"We have been watching, and he has not come out this way," Lord Arundel said, "and as ye all know there is naught but a window high in the wall, which is grated."

The hounds were led to the doorway and loosed. They stood there, smelling the ground uneasily. Then urged into the small dark room they but backed out, crouching and whimpering.

"'Tis a strange thing, and I believe there is something supernatural about it," said Lord ArundeL

"'Tis indeed an uneasy spirit which takes that form in coming back to earth.

I for one do not like it," agreed another.

"Who dares to go in and grope about?" suggested Lord Arundel.

"Not I, not I," said one after another.

"This isn't the first time we have seen the hare."

"There is something uncanny about it."

"Even the dogs seem to know it."

"Wilt thou go in?" and Lord Arundel turned to Tod.

"And why not?" assented Tod. "It was naught but a large, sleek hare as I saw it."

The youths shook their heads, and looked with admiration upon Tod as he strode into the dark recess. In a short space he returned. "Did it come out again?"

"Nay," they all said at once.

"'Tis not there, forsooth," announced Tod, "of that I am sure, for I walked around the room and groped with my hands into each and every dim part."

"'Tis always when we are the merriest that it does come racing along and trip us up. I do not know how many times I have had it run between my legs and send me sprawling!" said Lord Arundel, brushing the dust from the knees of his hunting suit as he spoke.

"It does seem to begrudge us sport!" said another.

"I have always said the castle was haunted," announced a third, who had from the beginning hung in the background as if he did not at all like the turn things were taking and dreaded to have them investigated. "If ye will take my advice, ye will all cross yourselves and say a prayer for the soul of the man whose spirit is not laid to rest."

Slightly subdued by this happening, which was one which was wont to take place at Castle Bolingbroke, and gave it the name of being a haunted castle, the party continued outside the castle walls, across the moat filled thickly with giant lily pads where the frogs sat sunning themselves, and which later would glisten with a host of golden-hearted lilies, to the tilting field. Here a group of young squires were busy practicing at the quintain.

The quintain was a crossbar turning upon a pivot, with a broad part to strike against with the lance on one side, and a bag of sand hanging from the other. In running at this it was necessary for the knight to direct his lance with great skill, for if it was struck wide of the center, the crossbar would turn about with great velocity, and the bag of sand would give him a severe blow upon the back.

"Wouldst try thy hand at that?" Lord Arundel asked Tod.

"Nay," answered Tod, "but I do think that if thou wishest to tilt with me on yonder piece of water, I could hold my own against thee."

Beyond the tilting yard and through a beech copse lay a small sheet of water, the bright glitter of which had caught Tod's eye.

"Well and why not?" agreed Lord Arundel. "Of course thou art more at home riding a skiff than a horse, and I have some skill myself at water tilting."

"Ay, that he has. Thou hadst best look out!" cautioned one of the youths.

"With a good lance and shield and Tom True Tongue at the oars, I have naught to fear," answered Tod. "But he had best strip himself of his fine hunting suit."

"Never yet, except in thy mudhole, have I had cause to wish my clothes safe ashore," put in Lord Arundel.

"So be it then!" agreed Tod, "but do not blame me if the color runs after a ducking."

Out into the pond slipped the two skiffs, and the match began. Back and forth sped the boats, and erect and fearless stood the two combatants, thrusting and parrying.

"Upon mine honor!" muttered Lord Arundel, "'tis the first time I have met my match."

"'Tis the same with me!" answered Tod.

"By fair means or foul thou goest in this day," sang out Lord Arundel suddenly. He signaled to his boatman, then sprang lightly on to the edge of Tod's skiff. Over it went, as Lord Arundel sprang back again into his own boat, which his boatman turned quickly to meet him. It was a favorite trick of his, and skilfully accomplished.

The surprised Tod and Tom True Tongue came up, and shouts of laughter met their ears.

"If the means be foul, look to thyself!" called Tod, as he took great strokes toward the skiff where Lord Arundel stood leaning on his lance, his face wreathed in smiles, and with every appearance of triumph.

"To shore! To shore!" shouted Lord Arundel desperately to his oarsman, but it was too late. Out went Tod's great arm, over went the skiff, and the next moment Lord Arundel came puffing and blowing to the surface.

"Out upon thee!" he gasped. "My hunting suit will – alas! – be – fit – only – for a stableboy!"

The young men watching from the shore danced with delight.

"It but serves him right," they shouted gleefully.

"May he rise from this bath without stain," quoted one, irreverently referring to the bath that was part of the ceremony of knighthood, whereupon they all laughed the louder.

"Methinks it will turn him as green as a sapling in spring!" shouted another.

Meanwhile the skiffs were righted, and all were aboard once more making for the shore.

"Enough for this day!" Lord Arundel announced as he set foot on shore. "Let us eat and be merry, but do not let us spoil any more good garments. Egad! the last few days have robbed me of my clothes with the devastation of the Black Plague itself."

Late in the afternoon as Tod and Tom True Tongue were making their way homeward, Tod rubbed his stomach.

"Canst remember all we did have to eat?" he asked Tom True Tongue.

"I do remember the host of savory dishes, but it would be beyond me to put a name to them. I can close my eyes and smell the spices and the herbs that flavored the rich gravies, and for many a day my mouth will water at the thought of them."

"There were boar's head and swan and roasted rabbit and pork pies and teal and woodcock," and Tod sighed heavily, "and tarts and hot custards, but alackaday! I had forgot that it was on business that I came, and I come away with but a day of pleasure behind me."

"Will the business not keep?" asked Tom True Tongue.

"I have a feeling that it will not keep as long as I would have it."

"Canst thou not tell me what it is that bothers thee?"

"If thou wilt not tell any man, I will tell thee it in part at least. Dismas, the young rascal, did wrest the five keys of the town coffer from the five men that did hold them."

"Then Dismas did win the wager!" gasped Tom True Tongue. In his astonishment he dropped the oar, and the skiff which he had been poling carefully close to the bank was swept out into midstream where the current was swift and sent twirling like a leaf.

"Don't upset us!" cautioned Tod. "I have had moisture enough inside and out for one day."

Tom steadied the skiff and soon was past the worst of the danger.

"Then off he goes with the keys!" continued Tod.

"And how about the town funds?"

"They are safe in the coffer, of course!"

"Well, then, can they not burst the coffer open?"

"They can but for one reason — "

"And that — "

"Is that they be the set of fools that Dismas said they would be," and both Tod and Tom roared lustily.

"And so thou goest to Bolingbroke to tell Dismas that?" asked Tom.

"Ay," answered Tod, "to let him know that his foolery has worked and to take the keys back with me to the foolish townsfolk."

CHAPTER XI. MARFLETE AND SKILTON PLOT TOGETHER

IT was in the middle of May, and a time of warm days. The gossip had changed, for now it was of the great fair that was to be held on Corpus Christi Day. As soon as Dame Pinchbeck heard the news, she hurried to count the savings so carefully stowed away under the brick in the big fireplace. How much could she think of spending at this great festival? Such a chance as she would have to make fine purchases! She stooped over to remove the brick and take out the bag beneath. The brick fell from her hands as she raised them in dismay. The money bag was gone!

She sank down on the settle conveniently at hand, for indeed her knees would not support her. Just then Goodman Pinchbeck came rolling over the cobbles, his face as ruddy and beaming as his goodwife's was pale and distressed. He removed his clogs by the door, and stepped briskly into the room.

Dame Pinchbeck cleared her throat, for she could not find her voice, and Roger turned toward her, thinking something amiss in the absence of a ready flow of words.

"What now! What's amiss?" he said. "Thou dost look as if thou wert ill!"

"The money bag!" gasped Dame Pinchbeck huskily.

"Thou dost mean it is not there?" and he too removed the brick and looked into the hole beneath. "As empty as a peasant's hut on fair day!" he ejaculated.

"Fair day!" gasped Dame Pinchbeck. "Speak not of fair day! Here is our fair day coming, and we with never a farthing to spend. Thou seemest to take our loss lightly, forsooth."

"Dost think the chapman could have taken it?" But Roger did not turn to look at her, and there was a gleam of mischief in his eye as he said this.

"I know not what has happened. Indeed it seems to me strange things are happening all around us, and not a soul does aught but let his jaw fall in a silly way just as thou art doing now, forsooth." Dame Pinchbeck had found her voice again, and the rest had given it added power. "What have the men of the town done since they discovered that the coffer had been thieved? Naught indeed, save rub their chins and talk of putting their hands in their own pockets to make up the loss. Were I bailiff, I would have ransacked every crack and cranny of this old town and beat every man who looked stupid until he took up the hue and cry himself. Alackaday! dost think now that we have been robbed that I shall fold my arms and say 'So be it!' Not I. And come fair day, I shall have my moneys to spend, or shall attend a fine gathering at the gallows."

"Tut! tut!" expostulated Roger, good-naturedly. "My business is good, and given time, I shall fill the bag again. Sir Frederick is stirring up the business of shipbuilding, and my ropes are in great — "

"Sir Frederick! always Sir Frederick! Sir Frederick this and Sir Frederick that! There are others in this town think not so well of thy Sir Frederick. And more than that, thy ropes would do well enough were they to hang the thieves. If I did not know thee pretty well, Roger Pinchbeck, I would say thou wert easily led by the nose, but again I know thee to plant thy feet so that not even a floodtide could move thee."

"Come now, say naught of our loss, and thou shalt even have a surprise some day!"

"I do believe thou knowest something about it, more than thou hast said. Hast thou thyself taken the bag? Tell me that!"

"Nay, nay, do not fret thyself. It will do thee no good, and see, for thy fairing I have even this in my pouch," and he drew forth three silver pieces which he laid on the bench beside her. Without more words he betook himself to the workroom, where two young apprentices were at work separating great lengths of hemp and twisting them into rope by means of a large whirl, like a spinning wheel.

"Here, Stephen," he called to one of them. "They are ready for that coil of rope at the shipyard. Do thou fetch it thither in the barrow."

"Is it for Sir Frederick's ship?" asked Stephen, a bright-faced lad of fourteen or so, whose quick movements showed he had not a lazy bone in his stocky, well-shaped body.

"Ay, but do thou not delay to look her over to-day, for work presses us here and we have no time to waste."

"'Tis a fine ship she'll be, and I be glad that the ropes that I have handled will be the ones to sail her," Stephen said, as he set about carrying out Pinchbeck's orders. "Dost think Sir Frederick will let me have a venture in her? I have a small amount put by, and I can think of naught I had rather do than send it out in her to come back in a small part of her cargo."

"Ho! ho!" laughed Nathaniel, the second apprentice. "Dost think to be a second Dick Whittington, and some day mayhap mayor of London? Ho! ho! Why dost not send out that black-snouted pig of thine and mayhap it will make a fortune for thee, even as Dick Whittington's cat is said to have done?"

Stephen turned, and stuck out his tongue at Nathaniel. "Ho! ho! ay," he mimicked laughingly, "mayhap some day I may be mayor of Boston and I'll make thee crier that every one may hear thy bright sayings!"

"Stop thy bickering and be off!" shouted Pinchbeck, and off went Stephen, his barrow lurching and bouncing over the cobbles, and he whistling merrily.

Although the silver pieces and Pinchbeck's unconcern did something toward putting Dame Pinchbeck's worries to rest, still there was much that she did not understand, and what she did not understand, she did not let pass out of her mind, but she worked slowly at it much as a dog worries at a bone, knowing there to be marrow within. She set a great kettle of pork over the fire to stew in its rich gravy, while she deftly rolled out a lump of dough and prepared a deep kettle. In a short space the pork pie was thrust into the hot brick oven above a bed of red embers, and Dame Pinchbeck sat down at her spinning wheel to work while it cooked.

As she sat there, she heard men's voices outside. One she knew was that of Alan Marflete. She recognized the high-pitched tone of it, and the way it rose and fell in great unevenness. The high-pitched words reached her, but the lower ones were lost in the general medley of sounds. "Coffer heavy" were two words that she caught, and again in a moment the whole phrase, "same except for locks." She leaned forward slightly so that she could peer out through the low doorway. Marflete it was indeed, and his companion was Peter Skilton who lived over the way. Dame Pinchbeck had no fondness for Alan Marflete. With all his church-going and gifts to the convents, he was not a favorite in the town, and Dame Pinchbeck was not the only one who saw in his face a crafty smugness and a selfish calculating look.

"He has the need of prayers," Dame Pinchbeck thought, "and I doubt if even they can make an honest man of him. I wonder what is in his mind now."

The two men passed out of hearing, but outside the Skilton house they stopped.

"Art ready to undertake it?" Marflete asked.

"I have no fondness for Sir Frederick, for he watches me like a hawk to see that I do not get my wool for nothing."

"Has he ever suspected thee of dealings with that man Redfern?"

"Nay," answered Skilton, looking around uneasily. "See that thou dost not breathe aught of that. I thought to be involved last year when his dog was caught, for he was ready to own himself the master. Dost remember how the dog growled and acted surly with every one but Sir Frederick? Even a dog shows love for him. Thou and I stand alone in our dislike."

"Ay," muttered Marflete.

"If we, with the help of circumstances, can tighten the mesh around him now, I'll not be the one to hold off," and Skilton straightened up with purpose in the movement.

"But we must not be seen too often in consultation," cautioned Marflete. "Do we both think out a scheme and meet to-night."

"Ay," answered Skilton, "and make it in the lower mart yard after the sun is set."

Marflete moved on up the street, and Skilton disappeared into his house.

During the noontime meal Roger Pinchbeck eyed his wife curiously to see if she was still pondering on the incident of the morning, and she on her part watched him while she talked of other things. When the last pewter mug and wooden trencher were in their places on the shelf, Dame Pinchbeck betook herself off. It was to Dame Marflete's that she went, and here she found Dame Spayne and Dame Marflete with tongues already clacking.

"How now, friend," Dame Marflete greeted her. "We are indeed glad to see thee, for it is a long time since thou hast come this way, and we should like to hear what thou hast to say about the happenings in this town." Dame Marflete was a large-boned woman with a long neck. She spoke in a fretful way with a note of reproach in it, as if she rather held it up against Dame Pinchbeck that she should not have come to her sooner. This note was strengthened as she added, "But then belike thou hast been talking with those of better standing. Lady Tilney mayhap? I understand thou and thy goodman are much thought of by the Tilneys."

Dame Pinchbeck did not answer at once. She cared as little for Dame Marflete as she did for Alan Marflete, and it was such talk as this that she liked least, for be it said of Dame Pinchbeck that she had no envy of those with more worldly goods than she had. All she asked of her world was that it should not deprive her of what was hers by right, and if less fell to her lot than to that of some one else, she bore the more favored one no ill-will. It was otherwise with Dame Marflete, who went on in this wise:

"We were saying that it does not seem right that the Tilneys should have the finest wool for their spinning and dress themselves in satins and jewels, while the rest of us content ourselves as best we can with homemade stuffs and silver brooches."

"I would not change places with them now," put in Dame Spayne, "not for all the jewels in their coffers, or their silver plate either. Dark clouds are lowering over their house, and I should not be surprised to see it crumble into ruins about their heads."

"How so?" inquired Dame Pinchbeck. "What makes thee talk in such a fashion?"

Dame Spayne settled her kerchief around her pretty face and pouted a little. "From things my goodman has let drop it would seem as if there were much talk about Sir Frederick. He looks wan and anxious, too, and has not the air of well-being he was wont to have."

"I like facts," demanded Dame Pinchbeck. "Canst thou tell just what they say about him?"

Dame Marflete held up one bony hand, and beginning with the thumb she set about counting off. "First there be this shipbuilding he is about, and his friendship with this merchant from Lynn. The son has been over also, and looks no brighter or more promising a lad than our own Thomas, and many's the time we have asked that Thomas be taken on as apprentice there, and a likely match would he make for Johanna, but Sir Frederick cannot see it that way, and needs must go as far away as Lynn to find a youth to his liking, and our Thomas — "

"We are not talking of 'thy Thomas' now," interposed Dame Pinchbeck.

"Ay," assented Dame Spayne, "we all know thy Thomas."

Dame Marflete struck her forefinger. "Then there be the robbing of the coffer, and that all came about because they would not take my goodman's advice. He wished them to use a coffer that he has, a stronger one indeed, but the locks be different, and it was Sir Frederick who opposed it the most strongly."

Dame Pinchbeck's face took on a look of keener interest. "'Twas not the coffer with the queer key, was it?" she asked curiously.

Dame Marflete's face reddened. "What queer key dost thou mean? I know naught about a queer key. If thou meanest the one my goodman fashioned himself from an old sheep thigh a long time ago, that be of no use to any one and has disappeared this long time."

"And why did Sir Frederick oppose the use of thy coffer?" pursued Dame Pinchbeck.

"I know not, unless it could be less easily robbed perhaps," and Dame Marflete's tone insinuated much. "There are those who believe that Sir Frederick has spent more than he estimated on his ships, and he has not really enough to start them out. He wished some of his townsmen to go into the venture with him and put their savings into it. My goodman is one who will not be led in this wise, and of that I am sure."

Dame Spayne sighed. "I wish I could be as sure of my goodman, but he is not satisfied with small and sure earnings, but he would venture all he has with the hope of rolling up a big sum."

Dame Pinchbeck said nothing, but she had found out all and more than she had come for, and she was well content with her shrewdness.

That evening in the gray shadows of the mart yard Alan Marflete and Peter Skilton revealed their plan. They believed the town coffer to be unmolested. They could not explain the loss of the keys, but then, as Marflete pointed out, he had known keys to disappear in unaccountable ways before. He had made a key, carefully chipped, and rubbed it down out of a piece of sheep thigh, and it was made to turn the five locks of his own coffer, and a year ago it had mysteriously disappeared. The last time he had had it was in the very same place they were to-night during the rumpus about the sheep dog that was thought to be a sheep stealer.

"What I propose," went on Marflete, "is for us to exchange the coffers. We shall take the town coffer to my house, and there we can break it open, and we shall replace it with mine which I know to be empty."

Skilton grunted. "Thou art a clever rogue, art thou not? Thou didst think to have the town use thy coffer, for which thou didst make a key to keep thyself."

"Hist! thou art as much of a rogue thyself with thy smuggling of wool into the town, but let us not quarrel now, for by carrying out this plan we shall accomplish two things: we shall be the richer and Sir Frederick will never be cleared of suspicion."

"What I was considering," Skilton rejoined, "was – would it not be better to take the town coffer out of the town? We could open it and dispose of the chest, and the money we could bury at some marked spot. Take it to my cart, and I can drive out with it covered over with hides. I have a little business with Redfern the day after to-morrow, and am to meet him up beyond Kirkstead. But what if the keys should turn up after we have made the change in the coffers?"

"There is no danger," Marflete assured him. "It has been several weeks now and nothing has been done. What with the excitement of the fair, the robbery is all but forgot. There will be a council meeting to-morrow, and after that I will let thee know if it be safe to move."

CHAPTER XII.
THE MYSTERIOUS NOTE

As he had promised earlier, the next day Sir Frederick did take Johanna outside the town walls through the warehouses and past the traders' benches to where below the quay was the small shipyard. Johanna kept close to her father's side, for she was conscious of the eyes of the men upon her as she passed. She could not enjoy the sights she was seeing or ask the many questions she would have liked to ask, as she saw at close hand the many things she had so often looked at from the top of the garden wall – the barges, plying back and forth, the porters carrying great loads on their heads, and most of all, the cog or cargo ship, broadly built with blunt prow and stern, belonging to the Easterlings, which was riding at anchor in midstream and turning slightly in the strong current of the Lindis.

"That vessel has been here more than a month, has it not, Father?"

"Ay," he answered, "the shipmaster is named Ranolf, and I like not him or his crew. Methinks they are about some dishonest business, but I have my eye upon them, and do not think to let them smuggle any wool through. Already have I fined them somewhat for certain packs that were not weighed and sealed."

By this time they had reached the shipyard, and there, indeed, was the "White Swan" well under way. Now was Johanna free to ask questions, and she learned that it was a small ship, even for those times, for its hold would carry only one hundred and twenty-five tons of Bordeaux wine, for thus did they then measure the capacity of ships. There were some that could carry five hundred tons, but these were among the largest.

The "White Swan" had castles at stern and stem, and a kind of palisade was built up around these, and underneath were cabins for the sailormen.

"'Twill be ready soon, will it not, Father?" Johanna asked.

"Ay, for by July we must be ready to set sail."

"And where will she go?" asked Johanna.

"To the great fair at Novgorod," her father answered, "and she will carry good English wares, and return with a cargo of eastern wares, for at these great fairs East meets West."

"I would that I could go with her," sighed Johanna. "Is not Gilbert Branche to go with his father's ships?"

"Ay, that is the plan."

Passing back through the warehouses Johanna saw pack upon pack of wool and iron-bound chests. Sitting at tables were young apprentices working over large leather-bound books and reckoning accounts by means of counters. All of it was interesting, but here again were the traders, eyeing her and whispering as she passed. They were the Easterlings.

When Johanna reached home, she betook herself to the garden wall. As she climbed, she was aware of a rustling in the lower part of her sleeve, and after she had seated herself, she drew forth a piece of paper. Smoothing it out, she was astonished at the words she found written upon it. It was strangely written, but this was the substance of its message: 'If thou wouldst be of great help to thy father, do thou come to the foot of St. Botolph's steeple to-morrow night after the compline bell rings. Tell no one of thy coming or nothing will be gained.'

"Midnight at St. Botolph's steeple!" gasped Johanna, and her heart seemed to pound within her breast at the very thought. "I dare not!" she breathed. "What might become of me?" She turned and looked up at the steeple which stood out in light and shadow, and its lantern caught and gave back in a golden ray the reflection of the afternoon sun. The sight of its great strength and friendliness seemed to reassure her. "I would I knew what might be gained." Again she examined the scrap of paper. It had been folded into an irregular lump and was but a small piece torn from a larger one. The writing was large and clear. "But what am I to do?" Johanna questioned herself fearfully. "Creep out all alone at midnight? Alas! I dare not. And not tell anyone? But that I shall. I shall tell Caroline, and she shall go with me." Thus Johanna arrived at a quick decision. The idea of companionship gave her courage.

Meanwhile Sir Frederick attended a meeting of the town council in the Guild Hall. Sir Frederick was indeed changed. To-day as he sat in his place at the council table, he leaned his head back against the high-backed chair, and it was not until Hugh Witham called the meeting to order that he was able to bring his thoughts within the four paneled walls of the Guild Hall decorated with fine carving and richly embroidered banners. "I am indeed loath" – Hugh Witham cleared his throat and raised his eyes to the vaulted roof – "to question the integrity of any of our townsmen, much less one who has in the past given great service and comes of a distinguished family, but it is my unpleasant duty to put several plain questions to him. Sir Frederick, it is of thee I speak." All eyes were now turned on Sir Frederick, who was leaning forward in his chair,

SIR FREDERICK TOOK JOHANNA TO THE SHIPYARD.

suddenly aroused, as by a blow across the cheek, into consciousness of his surroundings. His face was pale, but there was no fear in it, only a great unbelief. "How now," he spoke quietly. "I do not understand the cause for this, but I would far rather have things stated to my face than talked of behind my back." "So I thought myself," agreed the bailiff. "So let us be outspoken. First of all, why hast thou taken up with a merchant of Lynn? Are there no keen enough men in Boston, that thou must go so far to find one to suit thee in business ability?"

"Nay," answered Sir Frederick, "Sir Richard Branche came to me, knowing that I was a merchant of some means. I thought well of his proposition and so joined with him. I did not seek him out."

"Thou didst not even seek advice from any of us here," resumed "Witham. "Why couldst thou not have been open with thy plans?"

"I may not have been open," agreed Sir Frederick, "but neither have I been secretive. It was merely a private venture which involved none but myself."

"Ah! that brings us to the second point. Does it not involve more than thyself when thou, a leading burgess of Boston and a king-appointed officer of the staple, leaguest thyself with a Merchant Adventurer who preys upon the great merchant league that the Crown recognizes and grants rights to?"

"Thou speakest of the Hanseatic League of course," answered Sir Frederick, "but canst thou not see that it is because the league can give the king ready money that it obtains these rights? It is not for the good of England."

"Dost thou know better of this thing than the king and his advisors?" It was Alan Marflete who now spoke and there was a sneer in his voice. "Hast thou ever seen the great steelyard in London, and dost thou think with a paltry ship or two to oppose this league that has so strong a hold right in our greatest center of commerce?"

Sir Frederick groaned and despair settled over his face. "I know, I know, it will take more than one or two men's efforts, and it will take years and years before the pressure is great enough to be felt, alas!"

"In the meantime thou dost endanger the welfare of thy town. Here have we asked and received permission to hold a great fair in order that we may fill our town coffer again, and if aught of thy sentiments reaches the king, he will likely recall the permission, and then what shall we do?"

"Nonsense," and Sir Frederick roared with scorn. "Whose idea was that, forsooth?"

"I do believe it was Alan Marflete who suggested that possibility," answered Hugh Witham.

Sir Frederick turned to Marflete. "Thou knowest there is no reason or likelihood in that."

"'Tis well to be cautious when we are in such need as we are now," and Marflete shifted uneasily in his chair.

"Next we do believe that thou hast come almost to an end of thy resources in this shipbuilding venture. Is this so?"

"That is mine own concern."

"'Tis thine own concern – hem – until the public funds are – hem – involved and then – " Alan Marflete stopped to clear his voice again, for his courage was beginning to fail him. Sir Frederick did not wait for more, but turned upon him in justified anger.

"If thou thinkest I would use one farthing of the public funds for my private enterprise, thou art maligning me beyond my endurance." Marflete did not look him in the eye, but shifted uneasily in his chair. Sir Frederick's tones were scathing. "Thou hast not the courage to say in plain words what thou wouldst insinuate with thy hemming and thy hawing, but I'll tell thee what I think of thee plainly enough. Thou are a trouble-maker and a liar."

All the members of the council sat in awe as Sir Frederick towered over the shrinking Marflete, but the bailiff rapped loudly on the table. "I did not call the council together to listen to loud words and quarreling," he said. "We have been outspoken indeed, and now that Sir Frederick understands the position he is in, I think it best to let things stand for a time, and I ask ye all to keep to yourselves what has been said here."

Sir Frederick sat back in his chair, still breathing hurriedly. "Time only will show how things do truly stand," he said.

Later, as he and Roger Pinchbeck walked together through the market place, Pinchbeck said, "Thou knowest that I have every faith in thee and thine undertakings, dost thou not?"

"Ay, Roger, for the minute that thou didst hear of what I was about, didst thou not come to me with thy savings and entrust every penny to me to do with as I thought best? Thou art a true friend, and when adversity comes to a man, it is such friendship as thine that does give him heart."

"Do not take all this talk hard," cautioned Roger Pinchbeck. "It will all blow over, and by midsummer thou wilt wonder what it was that ever gave thee a moment's worry, and when thy good ship comes back, then will all the townspeople shower thee with blessings, for it will bring honor and profit to all of them, little as they will deserve it."

"But, Roger, what canst thou make of it all? As I have said but now, I have little faith in Alan Marflete. It was for that reason that I did oppose the using of his coffer for the town funds last year, for I did believe there might be some secret device for opening it, known only to him. Dost think I do him wrong?"

"I know not," answered Roger Pinchbeck, "but I think with thee that he will bear a bit of watching."

"And now I do bethink me who could best do it without awaking suspicion. He is coming to-morrow and I can keep him here on pretext of business, and that is young Gilbert Branche. He is a keen lad, and has sound judgment for one of his years. I do think that he and thy smart apprentice lad, Stephen, could perhaps fathom things where we ourselves might miscalculate altogether."

"It is a good plan, and something may come of it, indeed."

Sir Frederick grasped Pinchbeck's hand and wrung it, and with that they parted. In spite of the vexatious council meeting Sir Frederick felt less troubled than he had been, but Johanna watched his careworn face and wished more than ever that she might be of help to him.

That night as Caroline assisted her at bedtime, Johanna broke the news to her.

"Caroline, art thou brave?"

"Nay, I do not think so," answered Caroline.

This was not a good beginning. "Then thou must be," announced Johanna with decision, "for to-morrow night thou must accompany me on a dangerous errand."

Caroline gasped. "A dangerous errand?" she stammered. "What meanest thou?"

"I must go after the compline bell to the foot of St. Botolph's steeple and thou art to go with me."

Caroline's face grew white and startled. "St. Botolph's steeple! Hast thou forgot that the Devil haunts that spot? Surely thou art making fun of me? Thou canst not mean it!"

"Ay, I mean it. The Devil will do us no harm. We shall creep out well wrapped in our dark cloaks, and thou must not get faint-hearted and weak-kneed, for all that thou needst do is to follow me. I cannot tell thee more. Thou hast a day to think about it, and to get thy courage up, but do not dare to tell a soul what we shall do, or all will be lost, and great harm may come of it. Remember now!" With these instructions Johanna dismissed the frightened Caroline, and crept into her canopied bed to sleep uneasily, and dream strange dreams, in which the events of the afternoon repeated themselves, and the live white swan in the garden became confused with its namesake, the "White Swan of Boston."

CHAPTER XIII. THE KIDNAPPING

BETWEEN Boston and Lincoln to the south, before the great tract of Sherwood Forest was reached, there was a rolling stretch of sheep land and here on one of the hillsides above the Lindis and well off from the highroad was a round hut of stone with a thatched roof, such as shepherds built for themselves. Before it stood the shepherd, a square-built man with a weather-hardened face and grizzled hair. Near him was a thickset, longhaired sheep dog with a fine head and intelligent eyes. He was watching his master intently as he leaned against his rude doorway and looked far off. The glance of the shepherd returned and fell upon the dog with a look of proud admiration. "Thou art too fine a dog for the life I have made thee lead, my Angus," he said aloud. The dog at the sound of his voice leaped to his side and laid his head against him, wagging his tail. "Thou art the keenest sheep dog in all of England, and here I have made thee a dishonest one."

Angus sank down on all fours and lifted his flat ears slightly.

"Thou hast driven out the sheep just as I have pointed them out to thee, the longest-wooled ones in a radius of twenty-five miles, and thou hast not missed one. These we have rounded up for the smugglers and now have they sheared them and are about to take off the wool to their ship. To-night must we meet them and receive our payment and then are we through for this year."

The heavy tail beat the ground. "Come, we may as well start, for it will soon be dark."

The shepherd picked up his staff and the dog sprang eagerly away, and then came circling back, clearing rock and brush in his delighted bounds. Down over the hillside they went, making their way toward the Lindis below Kirkstead, which lay about halfway between Boston and Lincoln.

Here the Lindis flowed between heavily wooded banks, and deep within the woods on the left shore was a smugglers' cave. The ground around the cave and the shrubbery gave evidence at once as to the object of their smuggling, for here and there were tufts of wool which had escaped from the packs and caught on sharp twigs. The sheep had been collected here and washed and sheared, and then scattered again over the sheep land by the clever Angus. It was work that had to be done largely at night, and it was due to Angus's skill that the smuggling had not been detected, for at this time when all the sheep were being rounded up for shearing and then set loose again, it was hard to trace lost sheep or discover the sheared ones that were returned again.

As the shepherd and Angus broke through into the clearing around the cave, Ranolf with three other Easterlings came in from the river. Their voices had reached the shepherd even before the men themselves came into sight, for they were raised in angry disagreement. Angus growled and sniffed the air.

"It would serve thee right if we were all caught and hung, since thou wouldst risk everything by this silly plot of thine to kidnap the girl. And all because thou wouldst wreak thy vengeance on the father. 'Tis not worth the risk thou takest."

"Tush!" It was Ranolf who spoke. "Dost think I cannot carry it out?"

"It will but delay our sailing, and as likely as not she will not come."

"Why wouldst thou not be content to hide her in the fens?" another one suggested. "Hand her over to this man Redfern and let him take care of her. Make it worth his while."

Ranolf grunted.

"Ay," said another. "I would rather delay the sailing long enough to put off upstream a way rather than carry her off with us, and be followed and caught in our misdeeds."

Still Ranolf only grunted. By this time they had joined Redfern and Angus.

"Well met, Redfern," Ranolf growled in his broken English. "To-morrow night will see us cleared of this spot, and glad will we be, too. Thou hast done well by us, thou and that fine dog of thine." Ranolf tried to pat Angus on the head, but Angus growled and backed away. He showed a great dislike for all the Easterlings.

"Wouldst like to earn a few marks more?" asked Ranolf.

"Ay," answered Redfern, a little sullenly.

"Thou canst if thou wilt do as I say," and Ranolf went close to him. "The rest of ye get about the business of loading the boats and waste no time, for we must get back long before daylight." Then he turned again to Redfern.

An hour later the boats were loaded, and Redfern and Angus stood on the bank as they were pushed off into midstream.

"To-morrow shortly after midnight a mile above the bridge. If we are not there within an hour, the game is up," called Ranolf.

Redfern did not answer, but turned and, with Angus at his heels, disappeared into the forest. The boats with their dark, bulky burdens fell into line, and silently crept along downstream.

The next day Johanna's mind was somewhat taken off her hazardous midnight project, for Gilbert Branche again appeared, and had much of interest to tell her, and much to hear. Several times during his visit it was on the tip of Johanna's tongue to tell him of the mysterious note, but each time she caught herself with the thought that, as he was to be in Boston several days working under her father's direction, it would be better to wait until she had found what was the outcome of her visit to the steeple, and then he might be able to help her. Moreover she would not have him think her fearful. The question of their betrothal did not come up at first, though often did Gilbert start to speak in boylike confusion. But Johanna, knowing what was likely to come, with sudden skill broke away from the silence into bits of gayety. She told of Dame Pinchbeck at market, and at great length of the various stories in connection with the loss of the keys, for of course Gilbert wished to know what had occurred since his last visit in regard to that. He was astonished at what Johanna told him.

"And was the coffer empty?"

"I know not," said Johanna, "but I suppose everything was taken. 'Twas locked again."

"And have they not had it burst open?"

"Nay, they do use another coffer, so I think my father said, for, with the keys of that one lost, the bailiff did not wish to have it in use. So it still stands as the thieves left it."

"That seems to me strange. They have simply taken it for granted that the money is gone entirely."

"Of course," said Johanna, "who would not suppose so? Mayhap thou thinkest the thieves did open it but to put more money in," and Johanna burst into a merry laugh.

Gilbert watched her with delight, for she did indeed look pretty when the dimples came and went in her full pink cheeks.

"Knowest thou, Johanna, what plan thy father and mine have for us?"

Johanna's cheek grew pinker. Out it was at last. "Ay," she answered, "my father did speak of it, but it is not for a long time yet, and not then if we do not wish it."

Gilbert's face became serious. "But thou wilt wish it, wilt thou not, Johanna?"

"Mayhap, but that I cannot say until the time comes," and Johanna straightened the folds, of her dress with a prim little gesture, and settled herself farther back on the window seat. "I shall be but fifteen in August, and no one knows what may happen in a year's time."

Lady Mathilda came down the broad staircase into the hall, and the conversation was interrupted. Soon, at Lady Mathilda's suggestion, the two young people were busily engaged over the chessboard with its fine set of ivory chessmen.

"Thou wilt surely beat me," said Gilbert as he set up his last pawn. "I am not a good player, and thou, I know, art sharp-eyed and quick-witted."

Johanna laughed. "I can sometimes get my father into a tight place that he needs must use all his wits to get out of. But I have yet really to checkmate him."

"Thou mayst have the first move," said Gilbert, "for then I can say that for that reason thou didst beat me!"

"Fie upon thee! Thou must not give up so soon. Thou dost not know," and Johanna started off the game by moving a pawn. "Besides, of course it does not really give an advantage, as thou knowest."

As the game proceeded, they grew silent except for expressions of surprise or dismay from one or the other, as pieces were unexpectedly endangered or captured.

"Watch thy queen!" warned Johanna, "she is in danger!"

Gilbert's brow was wrinkled up in perplexity. "Ay, but what can I do? I cannot interpose my knight, for that will leave my king in check."

"Stupid!" laughed Johanna, "I cannot have thee lose thy queen, so I shall help thee. Play thy castle so. Then I shall not take her, for I should but lose my own."

"Ay," said Gilbert with a sigh, "I knew thou wert a better player."

"Check!" was Johanna's only response. Gilbert moved the endangered king.

"Check again!"

"And next time checkmate!" groaned Gilbert.

"Ay, thou art indeed cornered, but never mind! Thou mayst play with me again, and then perhaps thou wilt have the luck."

After Gilbert had left and it drew near to bedtime, Johanna began to show signs of uneasiness. She leaned her face against the window and looked out into the garden.

"How dark it is getting!"

Sir Frederick laughed. "Why, how now, it is but barely dusk!"

"And will it get much darker than this?"

"Of course, of course, child. Hast thou never seen the blackness of midnight?"

Johanna looked at him in surprise. "Nay, for then am I a long time asleep."

With that she arose, and bidding her parents good night went up to her room. There Caroline awaited her. "Hast done everything I said?" demanded Johanna.

Caroline was trembling. "Ay, but surely thou hast given up thy wild idea."

"Nay," answered Johanna firmly. "'Tis not often adventures come our way, and we must take them as they come."

Thus spoke a foolish Johanna, but in the Tilney blood there was a recklessness and a love of adventure, and moreover she did honestly hope that she might find out something that would help her father. The whispers about his implication in the robbery had come to her ears, and knowing how unfounded they were, she marveled now that the loss of the key had come in a certain measure to shake her father's position. All was not as it should be, and here was her chance, perhaps, to help.

Late that night the Blackfriars chapel bell was still ringing, when two figures emerged from the Tilney gate and slipped silently along the garden wall. Then, crossing the alley quickly, they crept stealthily along and soon emerged beside the parish church. The market place was still and empty. Caroline clung to Johanna, and together they made their way directly to the foot of the steeple. There they stopped.

"There be nothing here, and it is very dark," whispered Caroline. "Let us fly back!"

Johanna turned, and as she did so, her foot hit against something. She stooped and her hand found the bunch of keys left there by Dismas. She picked them up, for she seemed to know what they were instinctively. "I knew there was a reason for coming. I felt – " But here there was a shriek from Caroline, and Johanna's words were muffled, for a darkness enveloped her, and she was lifted up.

When she next knew what was happening, she found herself in a small boat with Caroline weeping beside her. She had been almost suffocated in the heavy cloak that had been thrown around her, but the cool night air revived her. A man sat near them, and another was pulling hard at the oars.

"Where art thou taking us?" Johanna demanded in as bold a voice as she could summon up.

The man turned, and Johanna was indeed frightened when she made out in the darkness the form and features of one of the hated Easterlings whom she had seen about the town.

"Come, now, thou hadst best row back with us, or my father — "

The Easterling laughed. "Thy father will have more to think of now than his packs of wool. We were in good luck, were we not, Heinrich, for we caught two birds?"

"Ay," answered the other, "but we must hurry. The wind and tide are right for sailing."

Caroline's loud sobs next caught Johanna's attention. "Hush! hush! hush!" Johanna urged. "'Twill do thee no good!"

"They are going – to – sail – off – with – us," sobbed Caroline.

"Nonsense," whispered Johanna, "we are going up the river."

"I did hear them say something about sailing. I am sure I did."

"Anyway," whispered Johanna, "whatever happens, I have the keys! I have held them so tight that my fingers are sore."

Soon the rower made in for the shore, and the other man stepped out and pulled the boat in.

"Out with ye!"

The girls got unsteadily to their feet, and were lifted ashore. Caroline gave a great cry, as a large black animal came bounding toward them. It was Angus, and he was followed by Redfern. Angus sniffed around, and for a second Johanna felt a cold nose against her hand.

"There be two of them," said one of the Easterlings. "Good luck to thee!" and pushing the boat off, in another minute the Easterlings were gone.

"What wouldst thou do with us?" Johanna asked.

Redfern grunted. "How wouldst thou like to be lost in the fens?" Johanna gasped, and Caroline fell again to crying. "But if ye can walk, I'll take ye to a shelter, and there ye may rest what remains of the night. I have no grudge against ye."

Johanna took heart at these words. "Come, Caroline, we shall go with him, and in the morning we shall see what we shall do."

Redfern started off, and the girls followed along over the rough ground as well as they could. Angus walked beside them, wagging a friendly tail.

CHAPTER XIV. THE TOWN COFFER TAKES A RIDE

SIR FREDERICK'S expression of downright distrust and contempt only served to make Marflete more anxious than ever to carry out the scheme he and Skilton had devised. He reasoned within himself that there was little chance of detection, for the keys were certainly gone for good, and if, through bad fortune, anything should happen to their plans, Skilton was something of a dull wit and he, Marflete, could easily clear himself. The night following the council meeting and the very same night in which Johanna was carried off by the Easterlings, Marflete and Skilton again met in the mart yard early in the evening.

Gilbert Branche had left the Tilney house at dusk and was making his way back to the "Golden Fleece." He had had a talk with Sir Frederick after they had dined, and Sir Frederick had told him of his wish that he should keep his eyes open and discover if he could any extraordinary happenings that seemed to be going on in the town. Gilbert spoke of the possibility of the coffer still being untouched, but Sir Frederick was unconvinced.

"However," he admitted, "if I had had my way I should indeed have had the chest burst open. Witham is an honest man but very close. It would hurt him mightily to see a fine chest demolished and I believe he is in hope even now of finding the keys. I see him walking about with his eyes on the ground as if he believes he will some day pick them up, one here and one there." Sir

Frederick smiled grimly. "There were brains behind the taking of those keys. Of that I am sure."

Gilbert's mind was full of this conversation as he walked along, and chancing to see a dim, rather slinking, figure ahead of him making toward the lower end of town he decided to follow.

As Marflete, for it was indeed he, entered the mart yard, Skilton stepped out from behind one of the rude pens which had a rough shed at one end. Together they disappeared into the darkness of this shelter. Gilbert had followed unobserved, and creeping around at the back, pressed himself close against the back boarding. Even in this retreat Marflete and Skilton spoke in whispers, and Gilbert could not catch a word that conveyed anything whatever to him.

Gilbert waited until the two men left the mart yard, each taking a different direction, then he himself came out into the empty dark lane. Suddenly he was surprised to see another figure step out of the shadow beside him. He stopped short and waited. The other also stopped. After a moment it spoke.

"What art thou doing here?"

Gilbert was at a loss as to what to answer, but he looked closely into the face of the speaker.

"Who art thou?" he asked.

"Stephen, the apprentice to Roger Pinchbeck, the ropemaker, and thou art Gilbert Branche."

"Ay," answered Gilbert, "and now do I remember thee, for thou dost spend much time around the shipyard and the quay. What art thou doing here?"

"Listening, even as thou wert," answered Stephen, "but I wager I heard more from the roof than thou didst standing below."

"What didst thou hear?"

"If thou wilt come with me, thou wilt see strange happenings this night, and it may be that together we may be able to do something to thwart them."

Stephen led Gilbert by back alleys and dark ways through which they had to grope their way, to a small group of outhouses. It was not until they had climbed up into the loft of one of these that Stephen made any attempt at explanations.

"This place belongs to Skilton, the weaver," he explained when he and Gilbert had stretched themselves out on a pile of straw. "He was one of the two men we have just seen. The other was Alan Marflete."

"What are they scheming to do?" asked Gilbert in a whisper.

"Carry something out of town in Skilton's cart to-morrow morning early. I could not make out what it is to be, but I got that much of the plan. We shall watch here until they come and then we shall see what it is, forsooth."

The boys continued to talk in whispers. They had much to say about the nature of the plot that they were watching unfold, about the sea and ships, about a multitude of things. Time passed quickly but their words became less lively, and at last Stephen said, "It will do no harm for us to sleep a little, for they will wake us when they come."

It was almost daylight when they were aroused by sounds beneath them. Stephen sat up, and Gilbert, who was already stretched out with his eye to a knot hole, raised his head and put his finger on his lip. They peered down through the cracks. There was Skilton piling hides into his cart. Then instead of leaving the shed as the boys had thought, giving them the chance to investigate, he went into the stall beyond and set about putting the harness on the big work horse. The boys looked at each other. When the horse was fastened into the cart, Skilton did leave a moment to go into the house.

"Will there be time to go down and take a look?" asked Gilbert.

"Nay," cautioned Stephen. "We woke too late. To think that we slept when they came in earlier! Now we must follow him."

Skilton returned, and climbing on to the horse, rattled out into the yard and off toward Bridgegate.

Gilbert and Stephen scrambled quickly down, and dodging out between the hogsheads and barrels, climbed a wall at the back and took another alley toward the quay.

"We must take my boat," Stephen said, "and I think we may be able to overtake him."

"Didst notice the barrow that leaned against the wall of the shed?" asked Gilbert. "The wheel of it was wound in tufts of wool."

"That deadened the sound of it on the stones," Stephen replied. "What they brought in it must have been heavy."

Pushing the boat into the river, the boys set about making what speed they could upstream. "How do we know he will not get rid of what he has before we are able to overtake him?"

"I heard the place they plan to meet again," answered Stephen. "Skilton is going to Kirkstead where he has business, but he will stop on his way back at a certain place beside the river. I know the place well. Here Marflete plans to meet him. He will ride out on horseback later."

"Then we shall make for that place and await their coming, shall we not?"

"Ay, we can conceal the boat and ourselves, if we make haste. It is much farther by the river, and will take a long time paddling against the current."

This same morning, when Johanna and Caroline awoke, light was just peeping in through the cracks in the hut. They had stumbled in only a few hours before, too weary and exhausted to do anything but fall down on the pile of rushes in the corner and fall asleep. Now Johanna sat up and looked around her while Caroline burst out again into sobbing.

Even as they sat there looking around in the dim light, discerning nothing but stone walls, rush-strewn floor, and a rude bench set near the open doorway, against the light of the doorway loomed a huge form. It was Angus.

Caroline buried her head in her arm to stifle a shriek, but Johanna jumped up. "Don't be silly, Caroline," she commanded. "It is only the dog, and he is quite the nicest dog I have ever seen. Come here," she called to him.

Angus walked over to them slowly and deliberately. Such a huge, clumsy creature he was that even Johanna was a little overcome by his proximity. "Good dog," she murmured, and put her hand out toward him. Angus sank down on his haunches at her feet, a great bulk of dog with bright eyes peering out from under a heavy crop of hair.

"He is so big," moaned Caroline. "If he should jump at us he would knock us over."

"He won't jump at us," scoffed Johanna. "Can't you see that he is making friends?"

Johanna knelt beside him and laid her hand on his head. Just then there was a low whistle outside. Up jumped Angus, and turning quickly toward the door, he did indeed brush against Johanna and sent her tumbling back over Caroline. She burst out laughing.

"He is such a big dog, and I am so little beside him," she laughed. Caroline raised herself on her elbow.

"And canst thou laugh even when we are in such a dangerous plight? Who knows what may happen to us to-day?"

Johanna sobered instantly. "I had almost forgot we were in trouble," she whispered. "Last night seems so far away and vague. Stumbling through the darkness with hardly a word spoken to us and then forgetfulness in sleep! Poor Father will soon wake to miss us! We must discover what this man is about. But the keys," exclaimed Johanna. "I had all but forgot them, too. They are hidden there in the corner." She felt over in the rushes and drew them out, then dropped them into hiding again. "We must get back with them!"

Jumping to her feet, she smoothed out her rumpled dress and moved hastily toward the door. Just outside was Redfern, but Johanna barely looked at him, so surprised was she at what she saw before her.

The sun was just rising in a bank of rose and gold, and the whole world seemed to be afire. Soft pink mist hung over the fens, and the silver river was aglow. Even the dull rocks of the hillside seemed to take on a rosy light.

"'Tis a glorious world, is it not?" said Johanna. "To think that I have never seen it like this before, nor like last night either."

Redfern looked at her, but did not speak. "Well now," continued Johanna, "what dost thou intend to do with us? Hast thou anything to keep us from starving?"

Redfern opened a bag by his side and produced two good slices of coarse dark bread. These he gave to Johanna. "There is water there," and he motioned to a clump of trees and a boulder.

Johanna was amazed at herself. She almost felt like singing as she ran through the ferns heavy with dew and drank the crystal-clear water. When she went back to the hut, she dragged Caroline forth. Angus was greatly interested and watched all her movements. Sometimes he followed so closely that it was as much as Johanna could do to keep from tumbling over him,

"What is thy dog's name?" she asked Redfern.

"Angus," was the short answer.

“He is friendly.”

“’Tis not always so,” Redfern admitted.

By this time Caroline had eaten, and feeling refreshed, she seemed to have forgotten her fears somewhat also. Redfern watched the two girls with interest, Caroline tear-stained and frowsled, Johanna with red cheeks and eyes glistening with excitement.

Johanna was sitting near Redfern with Angus close beside.

“Boston lies off there where the mist is the thickest, does it not?” asked Johanna. “Thou must take us back there, for they will miss us and be fearful. Should we not start immediately?”

“How much will thy father pay to get thee back?” Redfern asked suddenly.

“So that is what thou art after, a ransom for me ‘Tis not likely thou wilt get anything, for if thou hast been playing with those Easterlings, as belike thou hast, thou wouldst not dare to show thy face in Boston.”

Caroline’s face became full of consternation. “Nay, do not believe her. I do know her father would give a large sum to have her taken safely back.”

“Hush, Caroline,” warned Johanna. “Thou dost not know anything of what thou sayest. Leave this to me.”

“Thou hast a good deal of courage for thy size,” and Redfern looked Johanna over with growing admiration.

“I know thou canst not be entirely bad,” answered Johanna. “Thou hast a kindly look especially when thou dost look at Angus. Thou dost love thy dog.”

“Ay, he is the only friend I have.”

Angus seemed to know that he was speaking of him, for he raised his ears and looked over at his master.

“He has taken a strange liking to thee. Mostly he is surly with strangers. I understand it not. At a word from me he would be at the throat of any that I should so point out to him.” At these words Angus whined uneasily and raised himself so that his heavy muzzle rested against his master’s knee. “I’ll not put thee to the test, my Angus,” and Redfern rubbed his dog’s head roughly.

“I am not afraid,” asserted Johanna. “What sayest thou to this? If thy dog rush at me at thy command, then mayst thou take us back and get what ransom thou mayst ask, for I doubt not but my father will pay thee e’en though it should ruin him; but if he will not attack me, then must thou take us back safely for no payment."

"Thou art truly brave for such a little maid," Redfern answered. "I will do thee no harm and of that thou mayst rest assured."

"And thou wilt take us back at once?" pursued Johanna.

Redfern had become a changed person from the sullen, silent man he had earlier appeared to be. His grizzled face had softened and Johanna was surprised to see a smile lurking around his grim mouth.

"What is thy name?" Redfern asked.

"Johanna Tilney," was the prompt reply.

"Sayest thou so, and thy father, can thy father be Sir Frederick Tilney?"

"Ay," nodded Johanna.

"Is he Mayor of the Staple?"

"Ay."

"That dog is wiser than it is possible for us to understand. Now do I know that to be true."

"How is that?" asked Johanna.

"He must know thee to be a Tilney."

"And why should he?" asked Johanna curiously.

"Thy father saved his life, as the dog saved mine," Redfern answered shortly. "Canst thou remember a year past a dog was brought to trial for sheep stealing? 'Twas Angus, but by no sign would he admit me for his master. They could not make him pick me out from among the shepherds gathered there. Thus did he save my life. But when they could not find who was the master, one man suggested that the dog at least could be done away with. I was about to cry out, for I could not let aught happen to my Angus, when Sir Frederick stepped up beside the dog, and laying his hand on his head, he declared him to be too fine a dog to suffer for the misdeeds of a bad master. He spoke the truth. He is too fine a dog for such as I."

"Why, it is strange beyond belief," Johanna expostulated. "And is it true that thou hast aught to do with sheep stealing?"

The surly expression again returned to Redfern's face. "What I am and what my calling is has naught to do with it. Because thou art the daughter of Sir

Frederick Tilney I shall return ye both safe and ask no ransom."

So saying, Redfern picked up his staff, blew on his fingers a sharp whistle that brought Angus quickly to heel, and with a curt "Follow me!" strode off. Johanna and Caroline followed, still wondering at the strangeness of the outcome of their adventure.

Johanna was even gay now, and she enjoyed to the utmost the flowers and ferns that grew in abundance along the way. It was a marvelous adventure, and Angus was no small part of it all. Redfern delighted in showing off the dog's great intelligence. He would drop his staff unnoticed by Angus, walk on a considerable distance, and then order him off to find it. A short time Angus would be gone, and then he would surely return, the staff in his mouth, and he plunging through the woods in a great elastic gallop.

It was not until some distance had been covered that Johanna had a sudden and most disturbing thought. The keys! She had left them behind, concealed in the rushes in the shepherd's hut. How stupid that she should have forgotten them so entirely! What could she do now? Certainly Redfern would not return, and was it wise to tell him how important they were? How she wished that she might send Angus back to get them for her! This was a good thought. She hurriedly caught up with Redfern.

"I have left something important in the hut," she informed him breathlessly. "Dost think – would it be possible that Angus — "

"Thou dost expect a good deal from that dog," laughed Redfern, pleased, however, that she did. "What hast thou left?"

"I have left a bunch of keys concealed in the rushes, and they are important – to my father," she added.

"We shall try him," agreed Redfern. He called the dog to him. He pointed to Johanna, then back to the hut, then motioned him away. Angus ran a short distance, then not seeming to understand fully, he returned and looked up at his master. Again Redfern went through the gestures. It was not until the third time that Angus seemed to be satisfied. Then he started off and did not come back again. The three of them sat down to wait.

The sun had traveled quite a way above the fens, and still there was no sign of the returning Angus. Johanna became uneasy. "Thou dost not think he would start with them perhaps, and drop them somewhere, somewhere where they could never be found?" she asked anxiously.

"I know not. It was thine idea to send him back. We must wait and see."

Five more minutes passed, and still no Angus. "Canst thou not now whistle for him?" suggested Johanna.

Redfern crooked his finger in his mouth and whistled. Still no dark form plunging through the underbrush was to be seen.

"It would have been better to leave them where they were," sighed Johanna. "Then I should have known where to send for them. Why am I so full of foolish notions?"

"Ay, why indeed?" Caroline echoed. "If it had not been for thy foolish notions, we would not now be here. Who but thou would have ever thought to creep out in the dead of night?"

"Courage is apt to lead us into hazards," asserted Redfern, "and it takes a bold man to be a bad one."

"Art thou a bad one?" asked Johanna. "I do not think thou art as bad as that Easterling who did kidnap us; and it was he, was it not, who did tell thee to hold my father up for a ransom?"

"He did not say it was Sir Frederick Tilney who was to suffer. All he said was that thy father was Mayor of the Staple, and told me that if I used my wits, I could get a goodly sum for taking thee. I could say that I had rescued thee from him."

"And that thou didst do. It makes me tremble to think what might have happened to us. I am sure my father will want to reward thee well."

"Nay, I shall take no reward, for have I not already said that I owe him much? See! Here comes Angus! I hear him running through the crisp dry leaves."

In another moment Angus burst into view. He did indeed have something in his mouth. They all, even Caroline, who showed interest in spite of her dulling weariness, hurried to meet him. He sprang over the intervening space and fell on his haunches, dropping what he held in his mouth at Johanna's feet.

It was not the bunch of keys that lay there, but a large bone, which had been curiously shaped and chipped at one end, so that it resembled a key. Johanna looked at it in amazement, for it seemed to her that it was indeed one of the keys in her bunch which had been changed to a different substance. Redfern burst into a great laugh.

"If that dog is not a clever one, I'll say there be no king in England. He carried that bone away with him the day he was allowed to go free. He walked out of the town with his great head in the air, well knowing that he had done his best for me that day." Redfern took the dog's heavy muzzle in his hand, and held it up so that he could look him in the eye. "Thou knewest how to save thy master, didst thou not? And now," he added, "off he goes, and digs it up again, and brings it to thee. He seems to remember that day, and this but goes to prove it."

Johanna picked up the great bone and held it in her hand. It was quite smooth and shiny, almost like a piece of ivory, when she had rubbed away the dirt that clung to it.

Caroline was quite scornful. "Throw it away, mistress," she urged. "'Tis naught but a dirty bone and not fit for thee to handle."

"Nay," answered Johanna, "for now I do bethink me it will do well enough for me to keep, that I may remember this adventure and Angus. As for the bunch of keys, my father can send back for them when I do tell him of them."

"How much longer will it be before we shall be home?" asked Caroline. "I am so footsore that it seems as if I could go no farther."

"I shall take ye to the path beside the Lindis whence ye can see your own housetop, belike, and there shall I leave ye to go on by yourselves," answered Redfern. "'Tis now but early morning, and it may be they have not yet come to miss ye."

"Nay," answered Johanna, "that cannot be, for we all be early risers, and by now the market place will be astir with the news, and my poor father and mother will be dazed with the horror of it. Come, let us hasten, even though our shoes are but poor protection to our bruised feet."

Even as she spoke, there came to them the pealing of the bell of St. Botolph's church.

CHAPTER XV.
THE UPROAR IN BOSTON

MEANWHILE what had been happening in Boston? A day had intervened since Dame Pinchbeck's call upon Dame Marflete, a day spent by Dame Pinchbeck in mulling over the various bits of information Dame Marflete had let drop. Now indeed she knew where the savings from their wallet had gone. Her goodman had risked them all in Sir Frederick's venture and had not seen fit to tell her of his purpose. Ah, well! if he would have his little conspiracy without saying aught to her, she might as well have one of her own without taking him into it. And hers? Hers had to do with what she had overheard Marflete say about his coffer. It puzzled her more than a little. Here was the town coffer robbed, and here was Marflete telling Skilton that his coffer was exactly the same except for the locks, and lastly, there was the strange key that Marflete had devised. There could not be two ways about it. Marflete was the thief. The strange key was not to open his coffer, but the town coffer. There seemed but one person to whom it occurred to her to relate her suspicions and that was Sir Frederick. In spite of the scoffing tone she had used to her goodman about him, she really held him in great esteem, and she knew that he was the one to whom she must go.

She had arrived at this conclusion and was leaving her house just as St. Botolph's bell began to peal loudly and unexpectedly.

"By all the saints above! What has happened now?" she ejaculated. "What has happened now?"

Such an alarm could only mean fire, flood, or a raid upon the town. Which could it be?

"Fire!" screamed Dame Pinchbeck with sudden decision, and grabbing up the leather bucket which always stood ready for this emergency, she ran as fast as her stout legs could carry her down the alley and toward the square.

From all sides people came running, calling, questioning, dodging, hurrying.

Children and pigs were underfoot. Men carried weapons, buckets, ropes, and staves. Women still had in their hands the article they held when the alarm came: a distaff, a long-handled ladle dripping grease, a brush broom, or even a butter churn. Some had taken time to pick out some cherished possession, an iron-wrought candlestick, a piece of silver or pewter plate. Into the market place all were pushing and jostling. It was not fire, it was not flood, it was kidnapping.

"Johanna Tilney! Johanna Tilney!" was passed from mouth to mouth. Every one arrived at the same conclusion almost at the same moment. "The Easterlings are gone! They must be followed." Slowly the facts got around from one group to another, for the voice of the crier who stood on the market cross was striving against heavy odds. Caroline, Gilbert, and Stephen were also missing. Volunteers were called for, to man the fastest ship at hand to pursue the Easterlings. Off to the quay ran those who could be of service, while those who could not, returned to their work, sobered, stunned with amazement, and greatly troubled. The women wept and wrung their hands.

Dame Pinchbeck did not follow the crowd that rushed down to the quay, but joined Dame Marflete and her son Thomas. Thomas was a lanky lad with large ears, who shuffled awkwardly as he walked, and was stammering in his excitement.

"And didst thou not volunteer?" Dame Pinchbeck asked him.

"I w-w-was not at h-hand," he stammered out, "b-b-but — "

"Nay," his mother went on for him, "but if that young Gilbert Branche be kidnapped, too, why should he not rescue her? He is such a bright lad, forsooth."

"And our lad Stephen, too," Dame Pinchbeck added with real distress in her voice. "They did pick the finest young people in Boston."

"All but my son Thomas now, Heaven be praised!" and Dame Marflete raised her eyes upward. "Thou belike didst outwit them. Canst remember any time when they did try to lay hands upon thee, lad?"

"Nay," began Thomas, "b-b-but — "

"I thought as much. Thou didst outwit them."

"I saw two men c-c-carrying something heavy in a b-b-barrow through our b-b-back — "

Dame Marflete sought to hush him without drawing Dame Pinchbeck's attention, but Dame Pinchbeck pricked up her ears, and Thomas, now that he had something to tell, was eager to continue. It was not often that he knew anything others would listen to.

"Last night?" Dame Pinchbeck pursued.

"Ay," answered Thomas, while Dame Marflete hastened her steps.

"And what didst thou do?"

"N-n-n-naught," answered Thomas.

"'Twas wise!" Dame Marflete interposed quickly. "If thou hadst done anything, it would have been foolhardy, and thou wouldst have been kidnapped too. Thou art wise beyond thy years!"

Dame Pinchbeck only sniffed.

"And what thinkest thou it was being carried in a barrow?" and she watched him closely as she spoke.

"I think 'twas a l-large c-c-coffer," stammered Thomas.

"Thou meanest it?" and Dame Pinchbeck almost shrieked in her excitement. "And didst thou not recognize the men that wheeled it?"

Dame Marflete caught her breath.

"N-n-nay, for it was very d-d-dark, and they did m-move c-c-close to the wall."

"Of course, there's not a doubt, but 'twas the Easterlings!" announced Dame Marflete, and here at the corner of the alley, she stopped suddenly, and laid a detaining hand on Thomas. She would light a candle here in thankfulness for his safety. Everywhere throughout the town there were images of saints or crucifixes set up to call forth devotional feelings in the passers-by. Dame Pinchbeck bowed her head, and then passed on.

"'Tis a foolish son knows not his own father, but he be foolish enough," she thought to herself, as she remembered the conversation she had heard outside her window. "'Twas Marflete and his coffer, but what was he about?"

This made still more to tell Sir Frederick, but since this new and terrible trouble, there was no use in seeking him out. Even now he was making ready to set sail after the Easterlings, but she must tell some one and that right away. It would have to be Roger. She found him alone in the workroom, where he had returned after the first excitement had died away.

"What hast thou to say now?" she demanded.

"I do truly believe the Devil is at work," Roger Pinchbeck replied grimly. "I do feel as if he were making us all dance until we be dizzy and fit only to fall in a heap and hold our heads!"

"Well, then, if that is the way thou dost feel, what hast thou to say to this new bewilderment?"

"New bewilderment!" and Roger Pinchbeck sank down heavily on a coil of rope.

"Would it be possible for two men to remove the town coffer from the Guild Hall?"

"The Easterlings again!" gasped Pinchbeck.

"Well, if the kidnapping be the work of the Easterlings, this, not so!" answered Dame Pinchbeck. "This be the work of two of our townsmen," and she proceeded with her story while Roger Pinchbeck growled and grunted beneath his breath. "I was about to go to thy Sir Frederick with the tale, but now I cannot. It will have to wait."

"Nay," burst out Pinchbeck, "I shall seek out that rascal Marflete, and see if I can get aught from him. Mayhap he knows something of this kidnapping, too. I would not put it beyond him."

Straightway to Marflete's house went Roger Pinchbeck. It was Thomas he found, but a different Thomas from that of the early morning. He looked sullen and fearful.

"So thou sayest that thou didst see two men last night wheeling a barrow with a coffer on it?" Pinchbeck asked him.

"Nay, nay," stammered Thomas, getting red to the very edges of his large ears. "I w-w-was but half-awake then, and there w-w-was no c-c-coffer and no b-b-barrow. 'Twas the Easterlings and, methinks, a k-k-keg of ale they were rolling. Taking it to their s-s-ship, they were. They need plenty to d-d-drink, as thou d-d-dost know, and I am sure now that that is w-w-what I did see."

"And who has made thee so sure?" asked Pinchbeck shrewdly, and he caught the stupid Thomas.

"My m-m-mother," stammered Thomas without taking thought. "At least I m-m-mean that I did tell my m-m-mother and she did t-t-tell me that I w-w-was m-mistaken — "

"And where is thy father?" asked Pinchbeck, losing patience.

"He is away this morning. He r-r-rode away early on h-h-horseback."

"'Twill be time enough when he returns," and Pinchbeck lumbered off, thoughtfully twirling his liripipe.

Meanwhile, shortly after they had heard the bell pealing out its alarm, the girls, Redfern, and Angus came out into the highway and within sight of the town below on the river. Redfern called Angus to his side. "We must leave thee here and no harm can come to thee between here and thy home."

"Why art thou afraid to come with us and receive the thanks that are thy due, even if thou wilt not take more?" asked Johanna, looking eagerly into Redfern's face.

"Hast thou forgot that Angus at least is known hereabouts, and his master is in ill repute?"

"Wilt thou not trust to me that no ill will come to thee? I am sure for what thou hast done now, the good people of Boston will forgive thee what thou mayest have done before."

Redfern shook his head. "Nay, we must be off, but good luck go with thee!"

"If ever thou or Angus have need of help such as I might give, remember thou hast only to ask it of me." Johanna patted Angus as she spoke.

"Ay," answered Redfern as he turned on his heel.

Not very long afterward the two weary girls gained Simon Gough's bridge, and Simon Gough himself came out of the gatehouse and hurried toward them.

"The whole town is talking of thee, and where hast thou been?" he asked all in one breath. "Sir Frederick is like one distracted, and the word is that the Easterlings must have gone off with thee, as their ship set sail this morning before the town was awake. Never since I kept the bridge have I known of such strange doings in the town."

"We have no strength to tell thee now, but we were kidnapped, and the Easterlings were indeed to blame. Spread the news that we are safe, and now we shall hasten on ere we do drop with fatigue."

The news did spread fast, and before the girls had reached the Tilney gate, there were heads thrust out of every door and lattice window with wonder and joy written on every good face, and questions filled the air at such a rate that they could only be answered by their own echo through the narrow alleys. Sir Frederick had not sailed but stopped the preparations and hurried home. It was not until they had eaten and bathed their tired bodies that the girls could bring themselves to a full account of their adventures. Sir Frederick and Lady Mathilda were so rejoiced at their safety and so appalled at the danger they had been through, that they could only understand the whole story after several retellings.

"And thou dost truly mean that thou didst find the keys at the foot of St. Botolph's steeple?"

"Ay, truly, Father," answered Johanna. "I was creeping close to the stonework, and I did stumble on them just a few moments before we were set upon by the Easterlings."

"Thou wast a brave child, but foolhardy, Johanna. Thou must never take such chances again," and Sir Frederick's tone was severe. "But now thou hast left the keys again in the shepherd's hut, and the hut — "

"Is high on the hillside above the Lindis, and such a beautiful place, Father."

"Poor child," moaned Lady Mathilda, "and thou didst walk all that way."

"Nay, Mother, thou must remember we were taken quite a distance in the boat by the Easterlings."

"However, it was a long rough way, and I hope thou wilt suffer no ill effects from it."

"Do not worry, Mother," Johanna answered. "As thou knowest, I am very strong, and after I have had a long sleep I shall be as fresh as ever I am. But, Father, dost thou not think it strange that Angus should have seemed to know that I belonged to thee and that thou wast his friend?"

"There are sheep dogs that are as keen as, if not keener than, human beings, and I knew him to be a rare one with his strong, straight limbs, his well-formed head, and intelligent eyes. I remember him well. I do not know that I have ever seen a more strikingly fine sheep dog."

"And I have not told thee of the bone he did bring me, when we sent him back thinking that he would perhaps find the keys I had left, and bring them. It seems more than a bone indeed," and Johanna found the bone and handed it to her father.

Sir Frederick examined it for a long space. Then he said, "I am glad thou didst have the wit to bring it with thee. There is no doubt there has been work put into this and it certainly resembles a key. I think it will be well if we speak to no one of the other keys until we have them safe in our hands. Then will be time enough to tell how we came by them."

"And Redfern, Father, what dost thou think he is?"

"I think he and his dog are a great help to the smugglers, but I am greatly indebted to them. As father of Johanna Tilney, I would befriend them, but as Mayor of the Staple, it would be my duty to bring them to justice."

"Then I am glad they did not come into the town with us," said Johanna, "for I do not wish harm to come to them."

"Art thou going to send to the hut for the keys?" asked Lady Mathilda.

"Ay," answered Sir Frederick, "but Redfern and Angus will be far away from these parts, if I am not greatly mistaken."

CHAPTER XVI. TOD OF THE FENS STEPS IN

FORTUNE was indeed favoring Skilton, for Redfern, upon leaving Johanna, remembered his appointment with Skilton. He returned to the hut on the hillside, and finding the bunch of keys, he took them with him, and went on toward Kirkstead.

"Skilton can return them to Sir Frederick Tilney and it will be the quickest way to get them to him," thought Redfern, "and as for Angus and me we have done with this part of the world and will get clear of it to-day."

When Redfern handed the keys to Skilton with the instructions to see that they got to Sir Frederick as soon as possible, Skilton had all he could do to conceal his surprise and delight, for he at once guessed his good fortune. He knew that he must show no interest, so he even went so far as to say that he did not wish Sir Frederick to know that he had anything to do with Redfern and his wool stealing.

"However, it may serve to get me into Sir Frederick's favor, so I will take the keys. But how hast thou come by them?" he asked curiously.

Redfern was not in a communicative mood. "Never mind that," he replied gruffly, "but do thou take them to him."

Skilton had left his hides at Kirkstead and taken on several bags of grain, and other bags which had been filled with wool by Redfern. With Angus growling at his heels, he settled up with Redfern, and then climbing hurriedly on to his horse's back, started off on his return journey. A short distance down the road he drew up, and looking in either direction to make sure that there was no one to spy upon him, he quickly slipped off the horse. Uncovering the coffer, he hastily fitted a key to the first lock. It was a harder task than he had anticipated to find the right key for the right lock, but after a few attempts the first one turned. Pausing again to look around him, he worked over the second. At last he had turned them all. The lid scraped on its hinges, and he had lifted it enough to look inside. There were money bags, and as he poked one after another of them, there was the sound of coin within.

His time was short, for he knew that even then Marflete was not far away, coming to meet him and help him burst open the coffer. Hastily lifting out the bags, he jumped to the ground, and picked up some heavy stones. These he put into the coffer, and closing the lid, set about locking it with feverish haste. Then with the money and his spade, he hurried off into the bushes through a rough bit of woodland that separated the highway from the river.

On the river, Gilbert and Stephen were still working at the oars. Stephen rested a moment and looked around him.

"Thou wilt think I am a noddy!" he broke out gloomily. "I have missed the place. We are now quite a way above it, and only a short distance around this bend is Kirkstead itself. Marry — "

"Hist!" cautioned Gilbert, pointing to the left bank. There back in the bushes they could see a man. He was bending over his task, and was working fast. It seemed as if he were trying to push a boulder back into place with desperate hurry.

Dipping the oar into the water quietly, Stephen brought the boat in to the bank, and the boys crouched low. Shortly afterward they heard the rattle of a cart on the highroad.

"That was Skilton," whispered Stephen. "He has outdone Marflete."

Quickly the boys made the boat fast and scrambled up through the scrubby undergrowth. They found the place without any difficulty, and putting their shoulders to the rock, they rolled it away. Earth was only thinly spread over the bags, and they pulled them out.

"It is the town money!" gasped Stephen and Gilbert in almost the same breath.

"What we must do now," said Gilbert, "is to get the bags to the boat, but first we must cover this spot, so that Skilton will not see that it has been touched, should he return soon."

The boys worked excitedly. They covered in the ground and moved the stone back into place. Then they turned to the money bags, whereupon they jumped with fright, for there, standing over them, as if he had risen out of them like the evil spirit of the base metal itself was a large figure in a tawny-colored jerkin and long leather leggings. He shook a great mop of hair from before his eyes, and looked first at the boys and then at the bags at his feet.

"What are ye about?" he asked gruffly.

Gilbert was the first to find his voice. "Do thou not dare to touch those bags!" he commanded. "There be two of us, and together we are a match for thee!"

The man laughed loudly. "I could pick both of ye up in one hand, as easily as I would two fledglings, but tell me what ye would do, and mayhap I will help and not hinder ye!"

As he spoke, he stooped down and opened one of the bags. Putting his hand in, he drew forth the bunch of five keys and a few silver pieces. "By all the saints of the Holy Church!" he gasped, "the money and the keys!"

As there seemed to be nothing else to do, the boys told of how they had followed Skilton and Marflete and overheard their plot to carry something out of the town.

"We never dreamed that it would be the town money!" explained Gilbert, "for that was supposed to have been taken long ago."

"But the keys?" questioned the stranger, "where did they come from?"

The boys shook their heads, for there was much in the whole adventure that mystified them.

"What do ye intend to do now?"

"Take the money back to Boston and tell Sir Frederick Tilney of how we came by it."

"A wise plan, but before ye finish, ye may be glad that I shall be on hand to help ye!"

"And who art thou?" asked Gilbert.

"Tod of the Fens and a friend of Sir Frederick Tilney."

"I have heard of thee often," said Stephen, "and I wonder now that I did not know thee, for thou art just as thou art said to be: to wit, bluff and brawny with a laugh that can be heard as far as the curlew's whistle and a shock of hair that blows freely in the wind."

"Come then," said Tod, "since ye know me so well, let us take to the river with our prize." Tod took the money bags in his skiff, and pushed off, the boys following closely in their boat.

Tod rowed for a short distance in silence. Then he rested on his oars and waited for the boys to come alongside. "It will not do for us to appear with these money bags and be met by the excited townspeople. There has been something astir in the town, for I remember to have heard St. Botolph's bell pealing in an unusual way early this morning, and without doubt the townspeople are out like bees swarming."

"What can be causing the commotion?" asked Gilbert.

"Perhaps they have missed the coffer," suggested Stephen.

"I think ye must return and leave me to manage the money bags," announced Tod.

Gilbert and Stephen looked at each other doubtfully.

"Sir Frederick must know of this before the rest of the town, and then he will tell us how to manage it all."

"And what will Sir Frederick do?"

"That ye must find out."

"And what story shall we tell when they do ask us where we have been?" asked Gilbert.

"Say ye have been adventuring in the fens. There be many a Boston lad that does that!"

Stephen nodded.

"Go straight to Sir Frederick and tell him your story. Then bring me word here," and Tod brought his boat into a small inlet, which was close to a large oak tree. "Ye can remember this place without trouble, can ye not?"

The boys looked around to take note of the spot, and then nodded.

"Pull briskly on your oars and make haste." With some misgivings which a parting look at Tod's honest, merry face seemed to dispel, the boys rowed fast, and soon beached their boat, and entered the town by Wormgate.

Meanwhile Skilton had covered the straight stretch of highway at a sharp pace, his mind in a turmoil as to how he would be able to deceive Marflete. The keys he had put into one of the bags, so he did not have those to conceal from him. He had carefully removed all traces of fresh dirt from his spade and rehearsed to himself the ejaculations of surprise and disappointment with which he would meet the sight of the rocks within the coffer.

At the appointed place Marflete was awaiting him impatiently. He was nervous and excited, and his temper, at no time even, was on a great strain.

"What has taken thee such a long time?" he demanded as Skilton drew up. "I have been wondering why thou couldst not have left the coffer here on thy way, and I could have spent this time forcing it open. Thou wouldst not trust me, eh?"

"Thou knowest why," answered Skilton. "It takes two of us to lift it out of the cart."

"Well, maybe so," Marflete admitted sullenly, "but let us be about it. I have tethered my horse well out of sight and have chosen the best place to do our work."

"Forsooth, it is heavy," groaned Marflete when the coffer struck against his shins as he walked awkwardly over the uneven ground. "Here, let it down here!"

With a sharp implement which Marflete produced, he worked at the hinges and soon pried them loose. Then gripping the edge of the lid, they both strained at it so that it yielded several inches.

Marflete eagerly peered in and groped around inside with one hand. He swore under his breath. "Naught but rocks!" he growled.

With a curse and a kick he rolled the coffer off from him. Then he turned upon Skilton. His anger was up and all reason had left him. Skilton's well rehearsed speeches had no place, for out went Marflete's arm, and he struck Skilton a great blow across the face which sent him staggering.

"Curses upon thee!" roared Marflete. "Take that for thy ill luck and mine and that! thou dull wit," and with a deft kick, he sent Skilton off after the coffer rolling away in the bushes. Then he strode off to where his horse was standing, and mounting, betook himself and his anger back over the road to Boston.

Skilton sat up in the bushes and rubbed his head. "A dull wit be I!" he muttered. "Not so dull but that I can get the best of thee!" and his battered face beamed with satisfaction. He picked himself up and stood for a second over the chest. "A dull wit be I!" he muttered again, and throwing out the stones, he swung the chest up on his shoulder, and crept down to the river.

Sir Frederick, now that Johanna was safe, left the house to go to the warehouses. All along the way he was stopped and questioned by the townsfolk. He learned of Gilbert's and Stephen's return, and when he reached the quay, there were Gilbert and Stephen themselves, the center of a group of apprentice lads who were telling them of the kidnapping and asking them to account for their own absence.

"May we have a word with thee, Sir Frederick?" asked Gilbert as calmly as he could, withdrawing Stephen and himself from the others. "We have a message for thee from Tod of the Fens," he whispered. "And wilt thou tell me of Johanna?"

The apprentice boys fell away before Sir Frederick's presence, and Gilbert and Stephen walked on with him to a quiet place inside the warehouse.

"Tod is too late with his message, if it has aught to do with smuggling," Sir Frederick said as they went. "As thou seest, the Easterlings have sailed. As for Johanna, she is safe, Heaven be praised!"

"Tod's message has naught to do with smuggling," Stephen put in, and then between them the boys poured into Sir Frederick's startled ears their whole adventure, closing with the words, "and now Tod is awaiting instructions from thee as to what he shall do with the town money."

"And the money had not been stolen!" gasped Sir Frederick at loss to comprehend. "At least until Marflete and Skilton did attempt it. How stupid we councilmen will appear! Marflete and Skilton must be watched, and the money returned. The secret must be kept by Tod of the Fens and us, but how to get the money into the coffer?" Sir Frederick mused out loud.

Finally it was decided that Stephen should go to make his peace with his master, and Gilbert should return with the message to Tod. The message was that Tod should bring in the bags at nightfall, and Stephen with his barrow would come down for a load of hemp. Concealed under the hemp, the bags could be taken into the town again. So far the plan went, and further steps would have to be worked out later.

"Ha! ha!" laughed Tod to himself, and then out loud he laughed. He was thinking as he lay under the great oak tree on the bank of the Lindis, awaiting the boys' return, by what a strange turn of Fate's wheel he had happened upon the boys when he, at Sir Frederick's instigation, had been out to catch Ranolf or the Easterlings at their smuggling.

"Dismas must hear of this," Tod mused. "They say that he is to be present at the great fair. Would that he could be at hand when the money is found again. How it would please him!" This set Tod to thinking harder.

When Gilbert returned, he did not find Tod where he expected. For a second he thought he had mistaken the place, but there could be no mistake. There was the big oak tree, and there in the soft mud of the bank were the unmistakable marks of the skiff, but there was no Tod.

Back to Boston went the crestfallen Gilbert, and at the news he brought, Sir Frederick burst out wrathfully, "He is a rogue and a thief, and to think that we trusted him! There is no doubt that he has made away with the money, for, of course, nothing could have been easier. Now he will not dare to show his face hereabouts again, and we indeed are no worse off than we have thought ourselves to have been this long time. Only we three are the wiser! But I am the worse off, for I have lost the master of my ship and her crew."

CHAPTER XVII. TOD IN DISREPUTE

IT was plain to Sir Frederick how Skilton had come by the keys, for, learning from Johanna that Redfern knew that they were in the hut, he was sure that Redfern had returned for them and passed them on to Skilton. "I have felt Skilton did not come by his wool honestly," thought Sir Frederick, "and this is clear proof that he has had dealings with Redfern. My hands are tied for the present, for I cannot prove it on him without disclosing this mystery of the town coffer; and can I say to Marflete and Skilton, 'Ye are guilty of thieving the town coffer,' when a coffer I cannot prove is not the town coffer stands empty in the Guild Hall, as the townspeople believe their coffer to be, and the money has been taken from Skilton, the thief, by another thief, and – " But here Sir Frederick surprised himself, for suddenly the humor of the affair broke over him, and he laughed out loud as he walked along. "Well! well! here am I laughing at a serious business, but I do seem to see that rogue, Tod of the Fens, with his ruddy face brimming over with laughter at the trick he has played, and there is something about him and his open countenance that I do seem to trust in spite of everything against it."

"Sir Frederick! Sir Frederick!" It was Dame Pinchbeck who called him as he passed her door. "Step in a moment, I beg thee. I would tell thee how thankful I am for Johanna's safe return, and it warms my heart to see thee with a smile upon thy face."

Sir Frederick entered the low doorway and smiled upon Dame Pinchbeck. "I supposed thou wert going to take me to task for taking thy Roger's savings.

Truly, I do believe that with my venture I shall triple them."

"Nay, nay, Sir Frederick," Dame Pinchbeck interposed. "I would not begrudge thee our savings even if thou couldst not triple them, but I did berate my goodman soundly," and Dame Pinchbeck spoke with satisfaction.

"'Tis for the good of his soul, I suppose."

"Ay," answered Dame Pinchbeck, "and that he may not forget me. But what I would tell thee of, is this," and she lowered her voice to a whisper. "Last night when Johanna was kidnapped, Marflete and Skilton did change the town coffer for the one that Marflete had."

"And what did they gain by that except to have one empty coffer in place of another?" said Sir Frederick, well assuming surprise, for he felt Dame Pinchbeck was not the best person to whom to tell all that he knew, and he thought in this way to put her suspicions to rest.

"We think, Roger and I, that they do plan to get at the money that does pour in during the fair. They count upon that coffer being used, and Marflete has devised a queer key which will turn all the locks!"

"What is this? A queer key!"

"Ay, made out of a bone, and he claims to have lost it, but we do not believe it."

"A queer key made out of a bone!" and Sir Frederick's expression changed suddenly as a thought struck him. Then he went on, "Thou didst well to warn me. I beg thee not to spread this, but we shall watch Marflete and Skilton closely, and await further developments."

When Sir Frederick reached home, which he did with more than usual alacrity, he took up again the sheep thigh which Johanna had brought and examined it. Then he went out shortly, taking it with him, and it was to the Guild Hall that he went.

In all parts of the town preparations were going on for the Corpus Christi Fair. It was a spring blossoming of the town that was about to take place, for, being a religious festival as well as a great commercial affair, it would penetrate into every crooked alley and past every Gothic entrance to the hearts of homes and religious houses, and out would come a grand procession of townspeople in the rich vestments of the trade guilds, and of friars and priests and high officers of the church, bearing in their midst elaborately wrought sacred emblems.

The Guild of Corpus Christi was preparing a miracle play which would be presented in different parts of the town from a stage on wheels. The stage for these plays was built in three tiers: the upper section for Heaven, and here cherubim would appear wrapped in wool to recite what was set down for them to say; the middle section was for the earthly players; and the lowest one was curtained off for the players' dressing-room or used for the lower regions if the play should require that the wicked be thrust into smoke and flames.

It was to the Corpus Christi Guild that the Pinchbecks belonged, and Goodman Pinchbeck was assigned the part of Abraham in the play of "Abraham and Isaac." Stephen had to appear as the angel sent from Heaven, and Isaac was none other than Thomas Marflete.

"I would I did not have to appear and save him from sacrifice," Stephen confided in Dame Pinchbeck.

"'Twould be as well to let him die methinks! And a good riddance it would be!"

"That may be," agreed Dame Pinchbeck, "but do thou appear as thou shouldst, else my goodman will forget his lines," and she fell to repeating them in a loud and monotonous tone of voice:

"My Lord to thee is my intent
Ever to be obedient.
That son that thou to me hast sent
Offer I will to thee

And fulfill thy commandment
With hearty will as I am kent.
High God, Lord Omnipotent,
Thy bidding done shall be."

"Ay," burst in Stephen, "and then does he make a sign as though he would strike off his head, and Isaac does look like the pasty-faced butcher's lad that he be, and then do I enter and take the sword by the end and stay it," and Stephen threw himself into the part and took on the position of the intervening angel.

"Thou hast something of a player in thee, Stephen," commented Dame Pinchbeck, watching him with interest, "but Roger Pinchbeck cannot even say his lines without hemming and hawing and mumbling over them. He does play the part of Abraham about as well as I would that of a cherub, dangling from the roof on a winch device."

Stephen burst into laughter at the thought of good Dame Pinchbeck thus performing.

"But here hast thou been running wild in the fens for the best part of the day, with Roger needing thee in the workshop, and thou with the spirit of freedom still clinging to thee so that thou canst not stay at thy work. Get thee back ere Roger regrets that he spared thee a whipping!"

Gilbert had yet to break the news to Stephen that Tod of the Fens had failed them. He had dined with Sir Frederick and stayed afterward to hear from Johanna about her midnight adventure. Both were tired and still excited so that the visit ended in a quarrel.

"What wast thou doing in the fens?" questioned Johanna.

"That I cannot tell thee," answered Gilbert, whereupon Johanna was silent. "But why didst thou not tell me yesterday about the mysterious note thou didst find?"

"That I cannot tell thee," Johanna mocked, and let the conversation stop there.

"Come now, Johanna," begged Gilbert, "do not be angry with me. Tell me everything that happened to thee!"

"Nay," answered Johanna pettishly, "I am tired of telling of it. When thou canst tell me of thy doings, then will be time enough."

"Then I had best leave thee," said Gilbert, rising, but hoping that Johanna would turn friendly and delay him.

"Ay," answered Johanna, looking down, "thou canst go back to Lynn for all that I shall do to keep thee!"

"Why, Johanna, and thou hast asked me to stay on for the great fair, and hast promised that thou wilt attend it with me!"

"I did it without thinking," replied Johanna haughtily, "but now that I do think, I think differently."

"Mayhap to-morrow when thou art not so tired, thou wilt think differently again."

"I am not tired," denied Johanna, knowing full well that she was indeed, and a catch in her voice belying her. "But I am tired of thee and thou canst go!" With these impolite words Johanna flashed by, turning her flushed face away from Gilbert as she passed him.

Gilbert hereupon sought Stephen in the workshop, where he had the good fortune to find him alone. One look at Gilbert's face told Stephen that something had gone wrong with their plans.

"Am I not to go down to meet Tod to-night?" questioned Stephen at once.

"Canst thou believe it, Stephen, Tod was not there when I returned! He had disappeared with the money bags."

"Not there? Not by the oak tree?"

"Nay, he did deceive us. He intended all along to get the money away from us and make off with it."

"I don't believe it," announced Stephen solemnly.

"Dost believe that I did miss the place then?"

"Nay, but for some good reason Tod did not stay. Tod of the Fens has no look of a thief."

"I would say that myself did I not know it to be otherwise," answered Gilbert.

"And what does Sir Frederick say?"

"Sir Frederick also says Tod is a rogue and a thief."

CHAPTER XVIII. CORPUS CHRISTI DAY

TOD, the rogue and thief, made his way a second time to Castle Bolingbroke and this time with greater success. Dismas had returned. "How now," he greeted Tod, when he was brought into his presence by a grinning page. "This is an unexpected pleasure. Canst tell me what has been happening in the town of Boston since last I was there?"

"I could tell thee better," answered Tod, "if thou wert Dismas and not Henry of Monmouth, Prince of Wales."

Prince Henry laughed. "And why not? I did enjoy the part. To the fens again, and Dismas I will be until I must appear at the great fair in mine own right. Watch for me to-night, for I shall come."

That evening Tod and his band waited and watched and suddenly their ears caught the sound of a voice singing. Nearer and nearer it came across the lake, and soon the words could be distinguished.

"The noble Moringer he smiled and then aloud did say,
He gathers wisdom that hath roamed this seven twelvemonths and a day."

"He comes!" they cried, jumping to their feet. "Dismas comes!" The singing stopped, and a halloo sounded which was answered by a chorus of halloos. The next minute Dismas was in their midst. To the amazement of the fenmen, Tod approached Dismas and fell on his knees before him. The rest of them followed suit although they likewise did nudge one another and wonder with

eyes outstarting.
"Come, come! 'Tis not Prince Henry who has come but Dismas. Have ye forgot?"
The fenmen stared, hardly able to comprehend the words he spoke.
"Stupids! stupids!" burst out Dismas, "up on your feet and close your gaping mouths. I say that I be Dismas!"
Tod rose and motioned to the others who also rose quickly, all but Tom True Tongue. He alone remained on his two knees, his hands stiffly by his side, his head thrown back, and his mouth open.
"And what ails him?" Dismas asked.
Wat poked him with a cudgel he held, and Tom scrambled quickly up, suddenly realizing that every eye was upon him. He grinned sheepishly and said, "Sir Popinjay was right. The day has surely come when I be Tom Tongue Tie!"
Dismas and the fenman laughed at the sight of his comically perplexed face.
"To the ducking stool thou shouldst go," said Dismas, "but I will let thee off, for I have been told of the drenching thou didst get. Ho! ho! I should have liked to be there. But let us waste no time! Tell me what has been happening since last I saw ye."
When Tod told of the Marflete and Skilton plot, Dismas's face became serious.
"But the money, where is it now?" he asked.
"Yonder in the hut," answered Tod.
"I can see my part is not yet finished," sighed Dismas, "but it will be worth anything to be at hand when the coffer is opened and the money is found again. It must be on Corpus Christi Day, and when the Prince of Wales looks on! How many days to fair day?"
"There be three, for it opens Thursday next," answered Tod.
"Quite enough!" said Dismas, "but I shall need the help of some of ye!"
The next morning Sir Frederick was waited upon by Tom True Tongue, for Tod did not dare to take upon himself the mission.
"So thou art from Tod of the Fens, the thief and the deceiver?"
"Nay," answered Tom, "if thou wilt hear me out thou wilt know I am from Tod of the Fens, thy servant and thy friend."
Sir Frederick did hear him out, and Tom True Tongue returned to the fens

bearing news which made Dismas's face become aglow with satisfaction.

"Dost know," said Dismas, "I shall never again try to stir up mischief. There be mischief enough in this world without our adding to it for pleasure."

"Ay, ay," answered Tod, "and now it is meet for thee to know that we are going to give up our idle lives and serve thee as loyal subjects. To the sea we go on a good English merchant ship!"

Dismas heard at length about Sir Frederick's venture and the "White Swan of Boston."

"This Sir Frederick is a man after mine own heart," he said, "and the Prince of Wales shall hear of him. But come, thou sayest he has a key to the coffer and can return the money if we get it safely to him?"

"Ay," answered Tom.

"But thou hast not told him of the part I shall play?"

"Nay," answered Tom True Tongue. "He thinks it be Tod of the Fens who has made the plan and he is glad that Marflete and Skilton will be uncovered in their hypocrisy."

"They will be uncovered, and I wager that they will turn pale with fright and will think that St. Botolph himself has found them out and brought the miracle to pass. And who will play the part of the astrologer?" he asked suddenly, "for 'tis only by the aid of astrology and alchemy that this event can be brought about. 'Tis a magician that we need!"

"Let Tom True Tongue here play the part! With thy coaching he can do it well enough!"

So it was decided that Tom True Tongue would play the part of the magician, and called upon even by his Royal Highness the Prince of Wales, he would perform before the townsfolk of Boston.

Corpus Christi Day dawned. Boston had not rested for weeks preceding, with its coming of merchandise and merchants, of beggars, mountebanks, and strolling players, of knights in armor ready to take part in the tournament, and of ladies in their gay litters. Now it was adorned with booths and pavilions, with tiers of seats around the tilting yard and the archery butts, with the gayly streamered Maypole, and, above all, with a canopied dais before the Guild Hall, where the Prince of Wales would take his station and see the great procession.

With him would be the lords and ladies of Boston, the high bailiff, and the leading men of the town.

Mass was said, and the great day had begun. The narrow streets had been washed and cleaned in readiness for the fine robes that would sweep over them: robes of white damask covered with flowers of silk and gold; of tawny damask embroidered with gold eagles and emblazoned arms; of green velvet with roses of gold; of blue velvet with golden birds and angels; of white, violet, gray, and red satin of Bruges, ornamented with gold devices. Such was the grand procession, and all the townsfolk were on tiptoe with exhilaration.

Prince Henry, richly clad in a scarlet robe with ermine trimmings, talked with Sir Frederick Tilney. He asked of the "White Swan of Boston," and Sir Frederick Tilney, highly pleased, spoke openly of his great hope for England on the sea. Prince Henry listened, for the seeds which later when he was King Henry V blossomed forth into an active interest in the English navy, were beginning now to put forth roots. Below them as they talked the square seethed with upturned faces under kerchief, hood, cowl, helmet, feathered cap, and glittering headdress. The sound of music filled the air, and even the gray spires and turrets of the town sparkled as if hung with jewels for the great occasion.

Prince Henry turned from Sir Frederick to the high bailiff. To him he spoke of the rumor of the theft of the town funds. What was the truth of the matter?

Hugh Witham spoke briefly. The keys were taken; the coffer was robbed; it was not unusual in this time when rogues were many.

"I have seen to-day a clever astrologer whom I have met elsewhere. 'Twould give me pleasure to have him bring his art to bear on this theft. Mayhap with his instruments he could discover what took place, and perhaps even disclose where the treasure now lies hidden. What sayest thou?"

Hugh Witham raised his eyebrows and shrugged his shoulders.

"If it would give thee pleasure, that is enough of a reason for employing him. We'll seek him out."

The word was passed below, and voices took up the message, and passed it on. "The astrologer with the long beard!" "The astrologer with the long beard!"

Shortly the crowd gave way before a black-gowned figure, clasping in his arms a motley collection of books, spheres, instruments, and bones, and ringing as he came his small hand bell. He was lifted up on to the front of the dais where he huddled, still clinging tightly to his strange paraphernalia. Prince Henry spoke to him, whereupon he scrambled to his knees.

"If thy skill be good for aught, do thou read on thy chart and tell us something of the theft from the town coffer, that occurred in this town two months past."

The astrologer bent his grizzled head. Then he retired to the edge of the dais.

"Order the town coffer here!" he requested in a deep sepulchral voice.

Out from the Guild Hall came the town coffer, and up on the dais it was

THE ASTROLOGER.

handed, while the crowd stood below, amazed at the unexpected proceedings. The astrologer muttered over his charts. Then he spoke again to the prince who turned to the high bailiff.

"Be there any two townsmen by the name of Marflete and Skilton? The astrologer wants them."

Again the word was passed, and over the heads of people came the kicking, struggling Alan Marflete and the pale, shaking Skilton. Room was made for them and they stood bewildered and shaking beside the coffer. By this time

the crowd was shouting and pushing. Prince Henry raised his hand for order.
"What have these two men to do with it?" Prince Henry asked the astrologer. But the astrologer only shook his head and returned to the reading of his conjuring book. Then taking up the bones, he advanced to the coffer. He placed one of them on top and rapped around the edges with another. Then to the locks he went and there was a grating sound as the bone passed from one to another. At this point Marflete shrieked, and jumped down from the dais, only to be caught by Tod of the Fens, who was standing below, and hoisted up in great terror. The astrologer raised the lid of the coffer.
The crowd surged forward. There were shouts from the other side of the market place. The Prince leaned over and held up in succession, one, two, three money bags.
He turned to the high bailiff, whose face was purple with amazement.
"Why, how now!" Prince Henry expostulated, "me-thought there was a theft."
Then letting the lid to the coffer fall, he sat down on it and burst into a great laugh.
"The money is there! The money is there!" shrieked the townsfolk, and seeing the prince rocking back and forth they took up the laughter, and the square rang with it.
When one wave after another had passed over, each one increasing as more people got over their dumb amazement and joined in, it was suddenly discovered that Marflete and Skilton and the astrologer had slipped away from the dais.
Prince Henry ordered the coffer back to the Guild Hall.
"Do thou remove the treasure from that chest," he commanded the high bailiff.
"The coffer is bewitched and must be burned forthwith. That is my command."
The high bailiff nodded, for his tongue was still stiff with stupefaction.
Gradually the pendulum of order swung back and the events progressed. The prince and his party came down from the dais and moved on to the banquet in the Guild Hall. The townsfolk talked of the happening until the minstrels began to compose songs, and then the townsfolk had to listen to their own stupidity being sung from laughing lips.
After, the great fair had run its course, each day the buying and merrymaking

increasing until the great climax was reached in the big tournament on the eighth and last day. After it was all over and the last gay party had clattered over the bridge, with laden mule train ambling on behind, Boston, like a jaded peacock, closed up its fine tail and settled back to being an ordinary bird again. Then it was discovered that Marflete and Skilton in the midst of the goings and comings had picked up their household and departed, never again to be seen or heard of in Boston, leaving behind them the unsolved mystery of their connection with the greater mystery of the keys of the town coffer.

Dame Pinchbeck did not hesitate now to tell everything she knew, but even what she could tell did not do much to clear the muddled heads. Not even Sir Frederick was entirely clear, for he was not able to understand the part the prince had played; but Tod of the Fens had got the farce in its entirety, and through him Prince Henry was able to see that for once his hand had stirred up a froth that was a long time settling.

Gilbert chaffed Johanna saying, "Did I not tell thee the money was in the coffer? And thou didst only laugh!"

"Ay," answered Johanna, "but thou dost not understand how it came to be, nor how the coffer was opened. There is much thou dost not understand."

"Ay," answered Gilbert thoughtfully, "I do truly think that only Tod of the Fens knows, and he will not tell."

"He is no longer Tod of the Fens but Tod of the 'White Swan of Boston.' But what didst thou think of Prince Henry?"

"I did like him mightily," responded Gilbert.

"I did also. He had a merry way with him, and my! how he did laugh. He is indeed a prince whom all men may love."

Simon Gough thought this also as he stood by his gate when the prince rode out, and looking into a laughing face with blue eyes deep-set under heavy eyebrows, he received from his hand a gold noble.

Before the end of June the "White Swan of Boston" started on her first voyage. Well laden was she with English-made wares, and the townsfolk turned out, and St. Botolph's bell rang, as the wind filled her sail on which the griffins of the Tilney arms stood out emblazoned in blue and gold. Sir Frederick, Lady Mathilda, Johanna, and Gilbert stood and watched her sail out of sight.

"And thou wilt see her again before we do," said Johanna to Gilbert.

"Ay," answered Gilbert, "I shall follow fast upon her heels in my father's ship. All the ships are to gather at Lynn and sail together in a fleet."

"'Twill be like a flock of great white swans," mused Johanna.

The voyage of the "White Swan" was successful. Tod of the Fens proved an able master, and his men a gallant crew. After a few years Johanna and Gilbert were happily married, and Sir Frederick Tilney took his place as one of that fine company of early Merchant Adventurers which strove unceasingly, and opened the way for England during the following centuries to expand to the west, and to found the New England of the New World. As for Prince Henry, he became King Henry V, and his people marveled that a madcap prince could make such a well-balanced king. Perhaps it was the very breadth of his experience that taught him most.

THE BALLAD OF THE MORINGER*

The noble Moringer, a powerful baron, is about to set out on a pilgrimage to the shrine of St. Thomas. Upon the eve of his departure he calls his vassals together and offers his castle, dominions, and lady to the one who will pledge himself to watch over them until the seven years of his pilgrimage are ended. His chamberlain declines, saying that seven days instead of seven years would be the longest time to which he would pledge himself, but the squire of the noble Moringer takes upon himself the trust, and the baron departs upon his pilgrimage. Seven years except for a day and a night pass, and the noble pilgrim is still far from home.

"It was the noble Moringer within an orchard slept,
When on the Baron's slumbering sense a boding vision crept,
And whispered in his ear a voice, "Tis time, Sir Knight, to wake,
Thy lady and thy heritage another master take.

"Thy tower another banner knows, thy steeds another rein,

* This ballad was found in the introduction to Sir Walter Scott's "The Betrothed" and is attributed by him to the fifteenth century.

And stoop them to another's will thy gallant vassal train;
And she, the lady of thy love, so faithful once and fair,
This night within thy father's hall, she weds Marstetten's heir.'"

The Moringer starts up, and prays to St. Thomas to help him in the great trouble that is about to befall him, whereupon St. Thomas performs a miracle for his devoted worshipper. The Moringer sleeps again and when he awakens, he is in a well-known spot on his own domain, on his right the castle of his forefathers, and on his left the mill.

"He leaned upon his pilgrim staff, and to the mill he drew,
So altered was his goodly form, that none their master knew,
The baron to the miller said, 'Good friend, for charity
Tell a poor pilgrim, in your land, what tidings there may be?'

"The miller answered him again – 'He knew of little news
Save that the lady of the land did a new bridegroom choose;
Her husband died in distant land, such is the constant word,
His death sits heavy on our souls, he was a worthy lord.

"'Of him I held the little mill, which wins me living free –
God rest the baron in his grave, he aye was kind to me!
And when St. Martin's tide comes round, and millers take their toll,
The priest that prays for Moringer shall have both cope and stole.'"

The baron proceeds to the castle, the gate of which is closed, while inside preparations are being made for the marriage feast. The pilgrim begs for admission in the name of the late Moringer, and the warder grants it to him.

"Then up the hall paced Moringer, his step was sad and slow;
It sat full heavy on his heart, none seemed their lord to know.
He sat him on a lowly bench, oppressed with woe and wrong;
Short while he sat, but ne'er to him seemed little space so long.

"Now spent was day, and feasting o'er, and come was evening hour,
The time was nigh, when new made brides retire to nuptial bower,
'Our castle's wont,' a bride's man said, 'hath been both firm and long –
No guest to harbour in our halls till he shall chant a song.'"

When thus called upon the disguised baron sang:

"'Chill flows the lay of frozen age,' 'twas thus the pilgrim sang,
'Nor golden meed, nor garment gay, unlocks his heavy tongue.
Once did I sit, thou bridegroom gay, at board as rich as thine,
And by my side as fair a bride, with all her charms, was mine.

"'But time traced furrows on my face, and I grew silver haired,
For locks of brown, and cheeks of youth, she left this brow and beard.
Once rich, but now a palmer poor, I tread life's latest stage,
And mingle with thy bridal mirth the lay of frozen age.'"

The lady, moved by this melancholy ditty, sent to the palmer a cup of wine. The palmer drank the wine, and slipping into the goblet his nuptial ring, he returned it to the lady requesting that she pledge her venerable guest.

"The ring hath caught the lady's eye, she views it close and near,
Then might you hear her shriek aloud, 'The Moringer is here!'
Then might you see her start from seat, while tears in torrents fell,
But if she wept from joy or woe the ladies best can tell.

"'Yes, here I claim the praise,' she said, 'to constant matrons due,
Who keep the troth that they have plight, so steadfastly and true;
For count the term whate'er you will, so that you count aright,
Seven twelvemonths and a day are out when bells toll twelve to-night.'

"It was the Marstetten then rose up, his falchion there he drew,

He kneeled before the Moringer, and down his weapon threw;
'My oath and knightly faith are broke,' these were the words he said.
'Then take, my liege, thy vassal's sword, and take thy vassal's head.'

"The noble Moringer he smiled, and then aloud did say,
'He gathers wisdom that hath roamed this seven twelvemonths and a day.
My daughter now hath fifteen years, fame speaks her sweet and fair;
I give her for the bride you lose, and name her for my heir.

"'The young bridegroom hath youthful bride, the old bridegroom the old,
Whose faith was kept till term and tide so punctually were told.
But blessings on the warder kind that oped my castle gate,
For had I come at morrow tide, I came a day too late.'"

CPSIA information can be obtained
at www.ICGtesting.com
Printed in the USA
LVHW111158290322
714617LV00008B/860